ALLERGIC
TO
FOOTBALL

ABOUT THE AUTHOR

When **Rainer** was 10, he wanted to be a footballer. He wanted to see England win the World Cup and Luton Town to win the First Division (now Premier League). He's still waiting for any of these things to happen. He lives in London with his football-hating wife, two children, a dog and a cat. This is his first novel.

ALLERGIC TO FOOTBALL

RAINER WISEMAN

WISE**WONG**

WiseWong Ltd, (Publishing)
Registered No: 09683892

First Published in Great Britain, 2022

Cover artwork by Bobby Birchall
Typeset by Bobby&Co

For Rudi and Tia

PROLOGUE

After French footballing pioneer Jules Rimet had invented the football World Cup, he asked one of his sculptor friends to create a dazzlingly beautiful trophy to symbolize the glory of winning what he hoped would become sport's greatest achievement.

A few months later, he was presented with a small, slender, solid gold statuette of Nike, the Greek Goddess of Victory. Sat on a yellow gold marble base, its gold wings were splayed out like sun rays at either side to give the trophy an elegant shape and make it look like it could take off at any time.

Grinning from ear to ear, Jules slapped his friend on the back, popped his shiny new trophy in his suitcase and set sail for Uruguay, who were to be the World Cup's first hosts. By 1938 the trophy had captivated the world's imagination. People wanted to know where it shopped, where it went on holiday and how it stayed so fresh looking. There was also speculation that it contained mystical powers and if you touched it, you'd become immortal. Others, who had touched it but later died, dismissed this myth as nonsense.

The first person to try to steal the trophy was Adolf Hitler A great art lover and all-round evil Nazi, he sent a troupe of heavily armed soldiers to pinch the coveted cup from the Italian football team. They searched everywhere except under the bed of the manager, who had hidden the World Cup in a shoe box.

Following many other failed attempts, it was finally stolen while on display in London in 1966. The nasty robbers held the world to ransom, demanding a huge sum of money to give the trophy back. Luckily, a little black and white dog called Pickles came to the rescue. While taking his owner out for a walk one morning, he discovered the World Cup wrapped in newspaper under a bush in his local park. Well done, Pickles! As a reward, he got to sit on the Queen's lap during the final at Wembley Stadium, where he barked with glee after watching Bobby Moore lift the trophy for England.

Aside from that brief interruption, the most dominant team in World Football were Brazil. After claiming their first title in 1958, they went on to win the cup again in 1962 and 1970, where they were given the Jules Rimet trophy to keep. A new World Cup trophy was designed for the 1974 tournament, and that's the one still played for today.

But what happened to the gleaming Jules Rimet Trophy? Well, it was placed in a bullet proof cabinet and stored deep down in the underbelly of the Brazilian FA's offices. There was no way anyone was going to take the trophy from Brazil!

How wrong they were. On the 19 December 1983, just 6 days before Christmas, two thieves, posing as cleaners, put down their mops and lifted their crowbars. Within seconds they had prized the cabinet away from the wall and ran off with the trophy sending the world's media once again into a frenzy. This time, the trophy wasn't found. The most famous trophy in the whole wide world vanished from the face of the earth and it has never been seen since that day.

All that was true.

All that follows is almost nearly true.

*'The first World Cup I remember was in 1950 when
I was nine or ten years old. My father was a soccer player,
and there was a big party and when Brazil lost to Uruguay,
I saw my father crying. I said, 'Don't cry Papa,
I will bring you the cup one day'.'*
PELE

*'I've never known anything like the feeling of
holding that trophy in my hands.'*
BOBBY MOORE

Chapter 1

James Eligus sat on the low wall at the back of the buzzing playground with his head buried inside his green polo t-shirt and fingers jammed into his ears. He was trying desperately not to hear cheering noises from the absurdly green playing field. Not only cheers, but shouts of 'goal!', or 'shoot!' or 'pass it, you doughnut.' They could all spell disaster. He concentrated on the thud of his heartbeat and tried putting a melody to it. Something fast, like a Ferrari. *'Quick, think, or I'll hear it again.'* Too late. Hot tingles flushed down his spine as a goal-scoring cheer wafted past his defences and switched on a bright neon sign shouting...

FLEURBLER!

He squeezed his eyes shut. *Fleurbler* was James' word for his unusual allergy, an allergy which, according to the doctor's letter might kill him. This is what the letter said:

> **Patient: James Eligus, age 8**
> **Dear James,**
> **I regret to inform you that, following our recent random tests, you have contracted an allergy to football.**

Under no circumstances must you participate, view, touch, or listen to any form of this sport, as the consequences could be fatal.
Yours sincerely,
Dr A Percival

Pretty serious, eh? For two years James had managed to avoid most footballing sounds: cheers, conversations, commentaries and kicks, by sticking his fingers in his ears. He closed his eyes or looked down whenever he knew people were playing football. He averted his gaze at football adverts on tv, scarves, replica shirts and merchandise of all shapes and sizes. It was a full-time job and meant he was constantly on high alert, especially as almost everyone else in his class loved it and played it and talked about football all the time.

He'd only told one other person about his allergy and that was Margot, from his class, who was sworn to eternal secrecy. He didn't want anyone else to know because it was just too embarrassing, and if school bully Shane Splatter ever found out, he'd never hear the end of it. But, with only two weeks to go 'til the end of his school life at St Mark's Primary, James was cautiously optimistic that his secret might stay a secret. All he needed to do was keep focussed.

The noise dissolved into a regular playground din, and he let out a little sigh of relief. Only a little one though because the threat was always there, like wasps at a picnic. He slowly removed his fingers and, like a slightly curious tortoise, popped his head out of his bottle green polo t-shirt into the harsh bright sunlight.

Two tall boys with short, cropped hair wandered past, giggling. These were the Buzzcut brothers. They were in the other Year Six class, and he wasn't sure of their real names, but they were big and strong and very good friends with Shane Splatter, which made them creatures to avoid.

'Look, it's the poor little boy who doesn't like noise!', sneered blonde Buzzcut.

Brown Buzzcut leaned in and shouted 'LOOZA!' Making 'L' shapes with their fingers to their foreheads and kicking their legs out from side to side, the boys peeled away in hysterics back into the crowd.

Stuff like that was bound to happen today, he figured. It had rained consistently for the last thirty-five days, meaning the whole school had been stuck indoors at lunchtimes. Great news for James because it meant no ball games. And it meant he could hang out in the library in a nice quiet little corner which was a guaranteed *Fleurbler*-free zone. Today, it was sunny and hot, and it felt as though all the kids in the playground had been set free, such was the zany excitement bouncing all around him.

Back went the fingers in his ears as another cheer wafted up from the playing field. He shifted position and looked above the weird, grassy roof of the new infants eco building. The sky was perfectly clear. All he could make out was wall to wall beautiful blue. Definitely no *Fleurblers* up there, although weren't the sun and moon and planets all round like…?

He screamed silently. *'Death words! Death words!'* He clawed at his tongue, slid off the wall and fell on his bum.

'Goal!'

He stumbled to his feet, shoved fingers in ears and looked up to the sky once again. *Planets can't be fleurblers,* he reasoned, *way too heavy. And the sun is too hot to kick.* His pulse slowed. He imagined himself in space, having all that space. No mean people. He could just float blissfully for eternity. Then, he spotted something hovering like a bird of prey over the playing field. It was a tiny object, glistening silver in the afternoon sun. It couldn't have been an aeroplane, he decided. It was way too tiny. A satellite then? Too small and too close to be one of them, and it was hovering. A UFO then. A mini-UFO?

He started walking across the playground, his head tilted skyward, like a sun worshipping zombie. Would it come down and say hello? Was it planning on lasering the school to smithereens? He hoped for the first thought but concluded that if it did want to zap anyone then they should set the lasers for Shane Splatter and his massive Lego brick head.

Chapter 2

Down on the playing field, Margot jogged back for the restart after scoring her ninth goal this lunchtime. She was easily the best player at St Mark's and the main reason the Year Six team had reached their first West London cup final coming up in two weeks' time. Margot could play anywhere; she was strong in the tackle, could land the ball on a crisp packet from fifty metres, and could out skill the trickiest of foxes, but her favourite position was attacking midfielder because there she could set up and score loads of goals. Born and raised in Glasgow, Margot had only joined St Mark's earlier this spring. Before then the team was rubbish. Now, they were on the verge of a first ever cup final win and every match was lined with scouts from right across Europe.

The only scouts Omar knew were the ones who met in a hut by the canal and seemed to go camping when it rained. He liked football, but mainly because everyone else liked it. He wasn't a bad player either. He was lightning fast and great at crossing, but just found it hard to stay focussed for longer than twenty seconds. He high-fived Margot and did a little jig while singing '9-2, 9-2, 9-2, 9-2!'.

'It's 10-1 Omar, but never mind. Let's see if we can get fifteen before the bell goes!', said Margot with a smile, scraping her hair back into a long ponytail.

Shane Splatter wasn't happy at all. In fact, he was fuming. So fuming it looked as though his Amazon box shaped head was about to erupt. Having grabbed the ball from behind the makeshift goal, he pointed an angry finger at his goalie. 'Are you blind, Banksy?'

Poor Banksy shielded his eyes and squinted. 'The sun's too bright. I can't see properly. I need sunglasses.'

Shane snarled. 'Sunglasses? You on holiday or summing?'

'No. But...'

Shane interrupted him. 'Shall I get you an inflatable unicorn? A sun lounger? Maybe a nice mocktail?

'No, Shane. It's just the glare.'

He grabbed the goalie's top and lifted him off the ground. 'It's just shut up and try saving the ball next time. Otherwise, the next thing you'll be trying to save will be your teeth!' Banksy whimpered. Shane growled, turned, and directed his anger across the pitch at his celebrating opponents. 'I'm gonna show you alllllllll!' he roared, dropping the ball at his feet, and charging at them like a hungry rhino.

Omar wanted to tackle him but at the same time didn't want to get hurt. Plus, there was a boy sat on the bank with an ice-cream and he wanted to know where he'd got it, so he ran off towards the touchline.

Margot shook her head. 'Come back Omar!' But it was too late. Shane was almost upon her. 'Concentrate on the ball, not the boulder.' The fearless girl told herself.

'SPLATTERRRR!' cried the hungry rhino. Margot braced herself, but as he went to shoot, his standing foot slipped on the turf, his balance gave way and he fell backwards. His ferociously swung right foot scooped the ball vertically skywards like a rocket. 'HOYERGH!!!' He said, landing on his back with a mighty DOOOF! The players gathered around him like a gaggle of junior doctors.

'In FIFA, he might score 80 for strength but he'd be in the low teens for shooting.' said Banksy.

'Is he dead?' said Omar, leaning over the patient. 'If you are, and you can hear me, can I have your quad bike?'

'Isn't Shane too big for a quad bike?' said Banksy.

'He's too big for a tank', said Margot.

'I heard that!' said Shane, groggily rising to his feet. 'Did I score?'

'You've got to be joking!' said Margot. 'That was the worst shot in the history of shots.'

'Shut up, Scotland', said Shane, rubbing the back of his head. 'So, where's my ball?' The players looked around scratching their heads. 'That's my favourite Champions League ball! If someone's nicked it, they're gonna be sorry!'

'Is that it, up there?' said Omar, pointing skywards. The others tilted their heads.

'YEAH!' said Shane, proudly. 'And look, it's still going up! I bet you Ronaldo couldn't hit it that high!'

The players watched, mouths gaping as the ball rose to a tiny spec in the sky. A few seconds later they could make out a faint whistle as the ball began falling. A few moments after that the whistle had grown to steam train levels as the ball plummeted down at alarming speed.

'It's heading for the playground!' cried Margot. 'We need to clear the area!'

The players, except for Shane – who had spotted a tiny silver shiny object in a different part of the sky - rushed up the grassy bank shouting and pointing at the missile ball. Confused, the playground pupils looked up to the sky. Five seconds later, the area was clear, the kids having retreated with excited screeches to the outer edges. All, that is, except for one small boy who seemed oblivious to the chaos. He too was gazing up at the sky but, crucially, he was facing away from the plummeting pink ball and looking at the same thing as Shane.

Margot raced up the bank onto the playground. 'Hey, little one, GET OUT THE WAY!' she cried, waving her hands around. The boy turned to face her, smiling innocently. She recognised his face instantly, but before she could do anything, the pink football crashed down and landed on James' head.

Chapter 3

THULP! The pink football let out a little deflated 'pffffffff' as it settled around his ears. Margot was first onto the scene as a curious circle started to take shape around him. 'Are you ok?' she asked, looking into his glazed eyes.

'Tiny alien on my head' said James.

'That's not an alien, it's a…' she hesitated, lowering him to his knees. This was a very delicate situation. James was allergic to football and a football was currently sitting on his head making a cosy new home for itself. Should she tell him the truth? Absolutely not. His brain would simply explode if she did. She decided a very small white lie was needed.

'A hat fell on your head' she said. 'A very heavy pink hat. I'm just going to take it off, ok?' Ignoring his faint grumbling, she grabbed the ball with both hands and pulled upwards.

'Ow.'

'It's stuck' she said, stepping back.

'Leave it, it's nice and warm' said James. The lids of his eyes were drooping. 'I feel a bit dizzy.'

Fortunately, at that point, Miss Buckwell, a bouncy young teaching assistant appeared. She loved fashion and was always colourfully dressed. Today she was sporting a pair of bright yellow trousers and orange t-shirt. 'I love the hat!' she yelped, pointing at his head. 'Upcycling is all the rage! Did you find it in a bin? May I try it on?'

Before either James or Margot could answer, she too had gripped the ball with both hands and pulled upwards.

'Ow!' said James, for the second time.

'That's a tight fit' Miss Buckwell admitted with a frown. Before she could cause James any more discomfort, Margot thought it was time to reveal the truth to the young teacher. She felt guilty doing so, knowing she was breaking a solemn promise, but these were desperate times and surely James would thank her in the end. Miss Buckwell's expression turned from bright to bewildered. 'Really?' she choked. I mean, REALLY?' Margot nodded slowly. 'I mean, my boyfriend says he's allergic to shopping, but I've never heard of anyone being allergic to foo...'

Margot nudged her just before she said the dreaded F-word. 'Sorry miss. He calls it...' she felt silly saying the word, 'Fleurbler.'

'Fler- what?' she said, confused.

There was a pause. Margot gulped. 'Fler- bler.'

Miss Buckwell looked puzzled, shook her head, explained that his problem was beyond her pay grade whatever that meant, and strode off towards the main entrance. Margot crouched down opposite her friend and took his face in her hands. He had gone very pale, and his eyes were flickering like butterfly wings. She decided the best thing to do to keep him awake was hold his eyelids open with her fingers and keep talking to him. The trouble was she didn't have anything to say that wasn't related to football.

'Erm,' she paused. 'Nice day today, isn't it? Really warm and sunny.'

Thankfully, just then, Omar interrupted with a tap on her shoulder.

'Alright?' he beamed excitedly, pacing from foot to foot.

'Not really' said Margot.

'What are you up to?'

'Just helping James.'

Omar nodded, 'Who's James?'

Margot looked to the sky, 'this boy here.'

'Nice.' He glanced at James and pulled out a stick of chewing gum. 'What is it? Like, fancy dress?'

'No' said Margot, trying to stay patient. 'Shane's ball landed on his head.'

Omar had a good chew of his gum. 'Cool.'

'You do know who this is, don't you?'

'Yeah, you said, his name's James.'

'He sits next to me on our table. Opposite you?'

Omar stared back at her, blankly. 'Does he?'

Yes, it's James Eligus!'

Omar shrugged.

Margot threw her hands out in frustration. 'Shane calls him 'TA Cup' because of the shape of his arms when he puts his fingers in his ears.'

Omar's eyes lit up. 'Oh, FA Cup. Why didn't you say?' Margot slapped a hand to her forehead and sighed heavily. Omar continued, 'he's boring and he never plays football.'

'There's a reason for that,' said Margot.

'Yeah, he's probably rubbish.'

'No.'

'What then?'

Margot went quiet for a moment. 'Promise you won't tell anyone?'

He murmured in agreement. She coughed nervously, fully aware that she was about to really betray her friend this time.

'Ok but listen. If I tell you, will you promise to help me get that ball off his head straight away?' Omar nodded. 'And do you super-promise never to tell a soul what you're about to hear?'

Omar tutted. 'YESSSS!'

'Alright, well, and don't laugh, but…' she hesitated, 'that boy, James…'

Omar interrupted, 'FA Cup.'

'Yes, whatever you want to call him. Well, he's…' she winced. 'He's allergic to football.' Omar burst into fits of laughter.

Chapter 4

James had settled into a numb kind of contentment. The gentle ringing in his ears was drowning out most of the playground sound and the haziness of his vision helped him feel cocooned in his own thoughts. He had absolutely no idea where he was, who he was or what day it was, but it didn't matter. In his delirious state, he was imagining the dull throb in his head was down to the baby alien hat filling his brain with cosmic superpowers.

Down on the playing field, Shane was puzzled. He'd been gazing into the sky for a while, his eyes fixed on what he thought was some kind of tiny military drone. The shiny silver thing had disappeared and now he wanted to know two things: where his ball was and why everyone had deserted him for the playground. He blustered up the hill, wiping the sweat from his brow, and bulldozed through the circle of kids until he reached the small clearing in the middle, which was where he found the answer to at least one of his questions. 'Why is FA Cup boy wearing a pink hat?' he barked.

Margot gave Omar a stern look; a look which said, 'don't you dare say a word'. But he didn't get the message. Instead, he turned to Shane and said brightly, 'he's allergic to football, no jokes.'

'What?!' said Shane, baring a set of crooked, yellow teeth.

Margot glared at Omar, who shrugged in apology, then continued. 'And that's not a hat he's wearing either. It's your football.'

Shane was flushed with fury. 'Such a little thief!' he snarled. Grabbing the ball with both hands, the giant boy dug his nails in and yanked with all his might, pulling James in every direction. 'Give it back!'

'Ow!'

'You're hurting him!' cried Margot.

'I WANT MY BALLLLL!'

'It's my alien hat!' said James.

POP.

James fell one way, Shane the other and the busted ball settled on the ground between them like a big pink Yorkshire pudding. James took one look at the ball and pointed at it with a shaky finger. 'Was that on my head?' he asked, quivering.

'What else did you think it was?' said Shane.

'A fleurbler, on my head! POISON! AAAAAARGH!' He screamed, clawing at his wild long matt of curly hair. A sudden sharp pain jabbed at his tummy while a dull throb pulsed around his head. This was it, he shuddered. He was going to drop dead in the playground in front of everyone. He'd literally die of embarrassment if that happened. He gazed giddily at the hundreds of gawping eyes staring back at him and stumbled to his feet. His legs felt like jelly, which was probably down to the poison. His only hope of survival was to get to the toilet and try to wash it away. But he needed to get through this crowd and now they were giggling at him and repeating the word 'Fleurbler'. He squinted beyond them, at the spire sitting proudly on top of the school building and clumsily began his quest towards it, knowing that below that were the entrance doors.

'You forgot your hat!' shouted one of the Buzzcuts.

'He's as white as a ghost' said someone else.

His fake smile was drying up under the sun, and his head felt like it was on fire. He couldn't feel legs now, they belonged to someone else. Luckily, it seemed this other person needed to get to the toilet too. At least his secret was safe. 'Good old Margot', he thought. She hadn't let him down. Then he heard a familiar voice call his name which stopped him in his tracks. It was Shane Splatter.

'Margot tells me you're allergic to football. Is that why you're running away to the toilet?'

He stumbled, as though Shane's words had shot him. A burst of laughter rang out from all around and he suddenly found himself being jostled like a rudderless ship from side to side. Shane continued, shouting for all to hear like a town crier in a fairy story. 'James Eligus is allergic to football everyone. ALLERGIC TO FOOTBALL!!!'

A great rolling swell of laughter now crashed into the small boy from all directions. All he could say was 'Excuse me,' as the sky darkened, his knees buckled, and then everything went black.

Chapter 5

James sat in the reception area by the school entrance, scratching his head like an irritated chimpanzee. He'd woken up while being carried along the corridor by his sporty teacher, Mr Smith. The pain in his head had been crazy. For a while he couldn't see straight, which made him feel sick, and it was only after Mrs De'Ath, the headteacher, had come into the first aid room and given him some water and a cold flannel that his condition improved.

Once he could speak normally again, he thought it was important to tell them about his allergy. But neither Mrs De'Ath nor Mr Smith seemed to believe him, saying he was just concussed. They said his head had taken a nasty blow which was bound to make him think differently for a while. When he protested, Mrs De'Ath clapped her hands with delight and said he was obviously feeling much perkier and well enough to go home.

Mrs Landers, the receptionist peered over the frame of her glasses and settled her cold eyes on him. 'Your auntie can't pick you up, says she's too busy. You'll have to wait there 'til one of the teachers can take you home.'

That's a big fat lie. James thought. *Auntie Sue doesn't have a job.* They sat in silence, James staring at the passing traffic through the glass door, wondering why Margot had betrayed him. Mrs Landers stared at her computer, wondering what to buy her niece for her birthday.

A few minutes later, the door swung open and in stepped Shane's grandad, the Australian TV host, Brett Splatter. 'G'day Mrs Landers!' he bowed, lowering his shiny bald head. 'Looking gorgeous as ever.' The confident old man flashed her a super white smile.

'Ooh Mr Splatter,' she blushed. 'Such a charmer.'

Brett Splatter was Hanwell's favourite and only seventy-year-old celebrity. He was the host of an antiques TV game show called 'Measure the Treasure', where guest panellists tried to guess the correct weight and worth of various trinkets found in lofts and bins. He also owned the only mansion in Hanwell, which he shared with Shane. It was a huge charcoal-grey stately home that loomed down on the rest of the town like a heavy cloud.

'I do my best.' he continued. His body seemed to be led by a long, pointy nose, like a sprinter dipping for the finish line. 'Can you tell young Shane I can't pick him up after school as I've...' The sheer surprise at seeing James made him stutter and his eyes bulge. 'Oh, master Eligus, what brings you out here? Bored with the classroom?' Just as he was about to reply, Mrs Landers butted in.

'He got hit on the head with a football.' James covered his ears. 'Now he thinks he's allergic to it.'

'Allergic to what?'

'Football.'

Brett Splatter burst out laughing.

'I know' she agreed, giggling. 'We think he might be a bit concussed.'

James jumped up, about to protest, but felt suddenly dizzy, so he sat back down again. 'It's not concussion' he said. 'I really am allergic to...' He couldn't say the word. 'I've even got a letter from the doctors. I'll bring it in. My auntie should have given it to you ages ago!'

Mrs Landers was now all pretend sympathy. She looked at Brett Splatter and they both pulled sad faces. 'You've had a nasty bang on the head, James, but you bring that letter in tomorrow if it helps.'

'Why's he sitting there?' said Brett Splatter, leaning over her desk.

'His auntie couldn't pick him up, so he's waiting for a teacher to take him home. School policy.'

'I can drop him off if it helps. I'm heading that way now.'

Mrs Landers looked gobsmacked. 'After all the pain his father caused you?'

James covered his face. The walls felt like they were closing in. He needed to get out of there, fast.

'It's all water under the bridge, isn't it James.' He ruffled James's head, which hurt in more ways than one. 'Firstly, it's not James' fault his father's a nasty thief. Secondly, justice has been done.'

James kept his head bowed. Would he get told off if he made a run for it? Possibly. But what was worse, more humiliation or a detention?

'You're such a modest and noble gentleman' said

the receptionist. 'If only more people were like you. Unfortunately, you can't take him home because you haven't got a letter from his carer.'

With a look of fake disappointment, the old man threw his hands out and muttered an apology. Then his phone went and with a nod to Mrs Landers, and a sly grin towards James, his nose led him outside to take the call.

Chapter 6

'Look after that noggin of yours' shouted Mr Smith, through the open window of his car. James looked confused. 'Your head, mate.' The boy nodded, still baffled, 'and I promise, no more football talk during lessons!' Mr Smith drove off, leaving James gazing in slight embarrassment at his house.

He lived halfway down a long, narrow street crammed with small houses built before the World Cup had been thought of. The one belonging to James looked like it hadn't been decorated since the last time Uruguay won it (1936). The once white paint around the windows was trying to escape, weeds had won the battle against the stony singles in the narrow front garden, and the front door, which had once been as bright and blue as Italy's home top, was now a bored and faded grey.

The first thing James did when he got indoors was find his allergy letter. Padding up the stairs to his bedroom, he slid open the drawer of his bedside table, sat on the edge of his bed and read it.

Patient: James Eligus, age 8
Dear James,
I regret to inform you that, following our recent

**random tests, you have contracted an allergy
to football.**

**Under no circumstances must you participate,
view, touch, or listen to any form of this sport,
as the consequences could be fatal.**

**Yours Sincerely,
Dr A Percival**

Satisfied that the letter was real, and he wasn't going
crazy, he folded it up, put it in the front section of his
rucksack and returned downstairs, leaning it against the
end of the sofa. The living room was long and narrow
and dark. The only light came from the TV where Brett
Splatter was asking one of his antiques experts if a hopeful
looking woman's toilet brush, apparently from the 1920s,
was worth 'serious wedge'. The blinds were shut and there
was a rank stench of stale sweat and sickly perfume in the
air.

Facing the TV, and slumped on the sofa like Jabba the
Hutt, was Auntie Sue. She was a very tubby woman with
stubby little limbs and four chins dangling under her chin.
The most striking thing about her was her tightly curled
bright orange hair; it was as though she'd sheared a sheep,
dipped it in clown dye and whacked it on top of her head.

'Where you been?' she demanded, pointing the remote
control at him.

'School,' he said, cheerfully.

'Don't get fresh with me, mister!'

'But auntie, I go there every day in the week.'

'You're skating on thin ice young man. Now get that window open now! I've been sweating me ringlets off all day!'

James rolled his eyes, scurried past the coffee table, pulled open the blinds and pushed open the big bay window.

'Agh!' she cried, shielding her eyes from the sudden brightness like a vampire. 'Too much light!'

'Sorry auntie.'

She blinked furiously, then leaned forward, 'And why is your head all red?'

James felt his tender brow, sticky with sweat. 'I had an accident. Sorry.'

'Don't 'sorry' me,' she croaked. 'You should be grateful I agreed to look after you. I didn't need to, you know. I had a perfectly good life before...'

'...coming here.' Whispered James under his breath. This was her favourite statement. She said it at least three times a day. He was used to it by now, but it still didn't make him feel very good about his situation.

Auntie Sue had moved in - all bluster and boom - after Dad had been sent to prison. James recalled her being quite a nice lady at first. But then his memory couldn't be entirely trustworthy. This period of his life was now something of a blur. His only real memory from that whole period was the police lady sitting him down and telling him Dad had been sent to jail for five years. James couldn't cope with the new reality without his father. His brain basically shut down and he stopped thinking for weeks on end. It was as though he'd ran out of batteries. He couldn't talk or think or enjoy anything. Even when the sun shone, he felt bad, sad, guilty and pointless.

Then he started suffering from bad stomach pains and a doctor was summoned. He was given a course of chalky medicine and the pain eased. The true diagnosis came a few weeks later in a letter explaining that he was allergic to football. The very next day they cleared the house of everything football related and over time, the belly aches went away. His mind, however, was still far from healthy.

The doctor sent him to a counsellor who said James needed something to motivate him, so Auntie Sue suggested he try some chores round the house, like washing up and vacuuming. This seemed to work. The cogs in his brain began whirring once more as he started focussing on his tasks, intent on doing the best job possible.

Taking full advantage of her new helper, Auntie Sue started leaving James daily 'to do' lists while she was at work. And then, just as he was getting better and preparing to go back to school, she packed up work with a rare 'tired' illness, and said he needed to do all the housework, because she didn't have the energy to clean any more. He should also pay the bills because she was rubbish with money.

I've had a right old day of it in 'ere!' she sighed heavily. 'First, I had the shopping bloke wake me up….'

James looked confused. 'But he wasn't due until one o'clock!'

She shrugged. 'Yeah, well.'

'Had you been asleep all that time?'

'I'm a busy woman!' she hissed.

'The pies and chips were frozen. Have you put any of it away?'

'Hmmm?'

'The shopping?'

'What am I, your slave?'

'No. But. Where is it?'

'Where the bloke left it. In the kitchen probably.' She yawned.

'But it will have all defrosted by now.' James dashed into the kitchen where he was greeted by a clump of soggy shopping bags sitting in a huge puddle.

'You should have been here then, shouldn't you' she barked after him. 'Lazy so and so.'

Chapter 7

It was a beautiful, warm, clear summer's night. The silver drone flew silently down the tree-lined street, slowing to a smooth halt outside James' front garden. The little old lady controlling the machine from her hotel room set the drone to invisible mode and lowered it smoothly outside his front door.

Dropping off Shane's invitation had given her the creeps. The Splatters lived in a huge, dark grey mansion on the top of a hill, surrounded by barbed wire, CCTV cameras and blinding security lights. The cameras twitched at the slightest wave of a leaf on the breeze, and scary gargoyles loomed down from tall columns, warning off anyone with the slightest hint of goodness in their heart.

In comparison, James' modest and slightly tatty house was positively inviting. He lived along a long road, where the narrow houses on either side all seemed to be squished close to one another. She guided the drone to give her a view of his house and smiled to herself as fond memories flooded back. Part of her wanted to be there, where the drone was, to surprise little James, share a cup of English tea and talk about old times but no, she needed to stick to the job. Plenty of time for that soon, hopefully.

With a quick stretch of the fingers, the drone swooped

down to face the letterbox. The faded blue front door had once been the same colour as the shorts worn by her beloved Brazilian team. The drone hovered for a moment, silently. Then, from the underside of its body, two silver flaps opened, and a pair of twig-like silver arms appeared with pincers for hands. One of the arms extended forward and pushed open the letterbox. The other had a small postcard pinched between its claws. With a series of mechanical jerks, it tossed the card through the opening and retreated inside the machine.

The word 'DELIVERED!' flashed across her screen, accompanied by a triumphant 'DA!'

She let out a sigh of relief and drew the joystick back to raise the drone skywards. However, instead of heading back to her base in central London, she couldn't resist the urge to check on her great friend's grandson. She guided the machine over the roof and into the back garden. She didn't want to intrude and knew she was doing something very wrong, so she kept the drone at a safe distance even though it was now in 'invisible mode'.

Luckily, James had left his curtains wide open. She zoomed in for a sneaky look. Records, stereo system, speakers. Her mind wandered. She had once danced to music from possibly that very record player after the boy's christening and wondered why it had been moved upstairs.

Something else struck her as being odd. There was a distinct lack of football stuff in the boy's room. The last time she saw James he was obsessed with soccer. His face had lit up after she'd handed him a Brazil shirt for his sixth birthday. That was the last time she had seen the boy and evidently much had changed. Maybe he didn't like football anymore?

Chapter 8

James was curled up on the end of his sofa watching a football match on the TV. Yes, a football match. This was a dream, after all. But he wasn't freaked out, which would have freaked him out if he'd been awake. In addition, he was wearing a football kit; the England away kit to be more precise: Red top, white shorts and long red socks that covered his knees. And it felt comfortable and soft and new and special. Double weird!

The lights were on in the front room and the curtains were drawn. He couldn't hear or smell anything, but the world felt brighter, and he was calm and happy. Happy? Watching football? What kind of nightmare was this?

His dad rushed into the room with a huge bowl of popcorn. He was tall and slim, with short ruffled brown hair and pale blue eyes. James seemed happy to see him. Dad silently perched on the edge of the sofa and pulled James close. He gestured to the screen as if the screen held all the answers. What if it did? A football match? Not just any football match, this was a World Cup Final between the Whites and the Reds.

They leaned forward like ski jumpers, stuffing chunks of popcorn into gaping mouths. The score was 2-2 and the match had gone into extra time. It was nail-biting stuff. Then the reds winger crossed the ball into the box. The big centre-forward pulled the ball down with his right foot and swung a ferocious shot towards goal. The ball crashed against the bar and rocketed straight down before being headed away by a white's defender. James and Dad jumped up in uncertain celebration. Popcorn rained down on the floor.

As the perspective shifted, James suddenly found himself in the stadium, looking down at the drama like a curious hawk. The referee marched over to the linesman to confer. All eyes were on him, and he wanted to show the world his best walk. The Reds and Whites glared on anxiously waiting for a verdict. Had the ball crossed the line? Was it a goal? Divots littered the chequered green turf. There was a buzz of opinions and questions that would linger for eternity. James held his breath and the world followed suit. Eventually the linesman nodded, and the referee pointed to the centre circle, confirming a goal to the Reds. The stadium erupted, the Whites surrounded the ref like a gaggle of angry geese and back in his living room, James hugged his dad. He felt his warmth and love and the world was perfect.

Then the scene changed, and James was alone again. He panicked for a moment, before dad wandered back into the room wearing different clothes: a black jacket, black jeans and even darker trainers. Paying no attention to the TV, his father crouched over a black holdall by his feet and began checking off the contents with a series of quick nods, rope, binoculars, black gloves, balaclava, hooks and a Swiss army knife.

James tried desperately to get his attention but bizarrely, when he tried to speak, great plumes of smoke wafted from his lips and hung in the air like dark clouds. He shouted and wailed for his father but the more he tried the thicker the cloud became. Smoke filled his lungs, he clutched his throat and fell to the floor.

Chapter 9

He woke with a start, thrashing at his duvet like a beetle on its back, all arms and legs and sheer panic. 'FLEURBLERS?!' he cried, then 'DADDY?! DADDY?!' He blinked furiously around his room, panting and sweating his way back to the real world. It was just a bad dream, he told himself. Yes. Catching his breath, he leaned across and flicked on the radio. With the same hand he grappled on the floor for his headphones and clumsily hooked them over his ears.

The dream haunted him, stubbornly refusing to dissolve. And this song was only making it worse. He took off the headphones, got out of the sweaty bed and moved over to the window. A few stars twinkled in the clear night sky.

Had it really been just a bad dream, or was that really the last time James saw his father before the robbery? Forgetting about his bruise, he rubbed his head and squeaked feebly. Ow! He'd forgotten so much from the last two years he couldn't separate fantasy from reality and whenever he tried, his brain always led him back to the same place; sat on the sofa with the policewoman holding his hand. He hated that memory because it brought back such sadness; so with a deep breath and a quick glance at the silhouetted rooftops he went downstairs to grab a glass of water from the kitchen.

On his return a few minutes later, he spotted something on the mat by the front door. Sleepily, he bent down and picked up a postcard, wondering whether postmen delivered during the night nowadays. He headed back up to his room, sat on the edge of his bed and flipped the card over. James gasped as a golden glow reflected onto his face.

He was looking at a gleaming image of the Jules Rimet trophy embossed with gold leaf. His eyes bulged. It was beautiful. On closer inspection, the stem of the cup was a sculpture of an angel, or goddess, standing proudly with her wings splayed out resting an octagonal cup on her head. As his fingers followed the curves of her wings, he suddenly felt like he'd seen this image before. A calming sensation washed over him like a warm bath. It was bizarre. Eagerly, he flipped the postcard over and read the following…

Dear James,
Congratulations! You have been invited
to compete in a top-secret competition for
the long lost and extremely valuable
JULES RIMET TROPHY.

Your first task is to go to www.freejulie.fleb
and follow the instructions. You have until
6pm today. Tell no-one else!

Good Luck.

It was addressed to HIM! He couldn't believe it. He'd never been sent any post before. And it was so beautiful. The thought crossed his mind that the trophy might be some kind of Fleurbler cup, but if that was the case, surely, he'd be writhing in agony by now. So, what was this Jules Rimet Trophy? And why had he been invited to win it?

The following morning, he woke up in a good mood, which didn't make sense. His head was bruised and tender, Shane was bound to tease him about his allergy, the rest of his class would probably whisper mean things behind his back, and Margot, he'd never talk to her again. But despite all those things, when he looked at his invitation he felt comforted.

He bounded downstairs and put the postcard in his bag next to his allergy letter for Mrs De'Ath. At lunchtime, he would sit at one of the computers in the library and do some research on the Jules Rimet Trophy. Wait. He rummaged through the bag. His allergy letter for Mrs De'Ath. Where was it? His heart raced. It should be there! He was certain he put it in there last night. Panicking, James tipped the bag on its head and shook it. Old tissues and pencil shavings and a pen and some paper clips dropped onto the carpet. He dug his hands into the side pockets but came out with nothing but dirty fingernails.

Auntie Sue lumbered into the living room with a screwed-up face like she was chewing on a lively stick insect. 'What was all that screaming last night?' she complained. 'And what are you doing making all that mess?'

James ignored her. 'Have you seen my allergy letter?' he asked, panicking. 'I put it in here after school yesterday.'

'No.' Her face screwed up even more. 'Why are you taking that letter to school, anyway?'

The words rattled out of his mouth like machine gun fire. 'No-one believes I'm allergic to fleurbler. And you never told them, so I'm taking my doctor's letter in to prove it. Oh, and thanks for not picking me up yesterday when my head was throbbing like one of Brett Splatter's game show buzzers!'

Auntie Sue didn't say anything. She shuffled awkwardly, watching James on all fours, cover his face in despair. She then lifted her chins indignantly and shuffled her huge weight towards the sofa.

'I'm sure I told the school' she mumbled, before slumping into the groaning sofa. With a loud blow of the nose and a mild grunt, she leaned forwards and took a loud slurp of her tea. 'It's cold,' she said, turning her head away in disgust.

James raised his arms in disbelief, shook his head and trundled into the kitchen to re-boil the kettle.

Chapter 10

'Defend! Get it out! Keeper! No! Aaaargh!'

With clenched teeth and white knuckles, Shane threw his PlayStation controller at the screen as the Tranmere Rovers striker wheeled away in celebration. 'This Barcelona team is useless!'

This was his third game of FIFA this morning and it was only 5.32am. It was the same most mornings. No-one seemed to mind. His parents were off on another cruise trip, his grandad was sound asleep. It was only Les and Brian, his grandad's security staff, that occasionally asked him not to start playing 'til later and they were a soft touch. He'd tell them to get lost, they'd whine from behind the door, he'd throw something at it, and they'd go away. Easy. Besides, he thought, it was good for him to spend as much time as possible playing video games. They helped him get to sleep at night (sometimes he'd play 'til 2am) and helped wake him up in the mornings. Also, sleep was for idiots and homework, which he never did, was for...idiots as well.

Shane's bedroom was a gamer's paradise. Along one wall was three giant paper-thin TVs. One for the Xbox, one for the PS5 and one for the Nintendo. Opposite each screen was a top of the range gaming chair and virtual reality headset. There was a knock on the door. 'Get lost!'

'Shaney? Everything ok?' asked Les.

'Do you need a hot milk and some biscuits to calm you down?' asked Brian.

Brian and Les had been Brett Splatter's live-in security guards since he moved into the mansion in the 1980s. They helped raise Brett's daughter, Sheila Splatter. They were very old page boys at her wedding, set up the east wing for the newlyweds to live in and were present at Shane's birth ten years ago. They babysat him; took him to nursery; had dropped him off on his first day of school; picked him up after he'd stuffed crayons up a small boy's nostrils and been sent home an hour later; brought him his first bike; brought him his second bike two days later after the first one was thrown under a moving car because it didn't work properly (he couldn't ride it); consoled him after his parents went away on their first cruise holiday without him; and second, and third, and fourth. The men loved him as their own and were utterly devoted to him.

'Of course he doesn't want hot milk, Les! It's too early!' boomed Brian. Then more softly.

'Would you like a nice cool glass of water, Shaney mate?'

Shane ran to the door and swung it open. 'Here!' He thrust the crushed and slightly smoking PlayStation controller at Brian. 'Get me a new one. This got broke!' And slammed the door shut.

Another knock followed. 'Shaney mate?' said Les,

apologetically. 'Don't you think it's a bit early to be on the games? You've got school this morning. Maybe go back to...'

Shane swung open the door once more.

'Get out of my face, now!' His voice softened. 'And bring some hot milk and bickies.'

'That's our Shaney!' said Les, smiling.

Slamming the door shut, Shane slumped on his enormous bed. His head was swimming, and he could see stars in the ceiling. Maybe he was tired. Maybe that's why he lost? His mind wandered to his parents waving goodbye in the back of his grandad's Rolls Royce. He imagined they were waving, anyway. The windows were blacked out. Was he missing his parents? He wondered. Definitely not. They obviously didn't miss him. He hadn't had a phone call since last week, he hadn't had any presents sent to him, he hadn't even had a postcard! He clenched his fists. His life was better without them, anyway, he decided. After all, he could play whatever video game he wanted, when he wanted, and he didn't have to bother caring about school or being nice or anything. Life was sweet! He jumped up, went over to the X-Box, and switched it on.

Chapter 11

At 7.23am, Shane traipsed into the kitchen and slumped down at the breakfast table. He let out a lion-sized yawn and frowned. He went to pick up his regular morning mug of hot chocolate but found a postcard leaning against the handle. Frowning, he picked it up and gazed at the writing on the back. The **'Dear Shane'** bit had been thoughtfully highlighted. Must be for him, then, he thought.

'Dear Shane' He mumbled, trying to read it. He blew out a sigh and rubbed his forehead. He was too hot to think, and besides, reading was for idiots. He flipped it over and was taken aback by a sudden flash of gold.

On the face of the postcard was an image of the Jules Rimet Trophy which, unbeknownst to him, was identical to the card sent to James. The shimmering gold trophy made his eyes light up like headlamps. He flipped the postcard over once again, wondering who could have sent it. It wasn't his Mum's handwriting; he was certain of that. Hers was swirly and posh and nice and made him think of Christmas and the quad bike she brought him last year.

He squinted at the typed words but could only make out some kind of website because he recognised the '@' and a number 6, which was his shirt number for the football team. 'Junk mail then' he decided. He took one more look

47

at the shiny gold trophy, because it looked pretty cool, and flipped the bin open.

'What are you doing?' cried Les and Brian, rushing in.

'What?'

'Don't throw it away! It's your big invitation!' said Les, excitedly.

'Eh?'

Brian took it from him and held it up. 'We've been waiting ages for this.'

Shane scratched his head. 'What are you talking about?'

'Remember those books we got you on the history of the World Cup?' said Les.

'No.'

'And all that extra football training we've been doing?' said Brian.

'I just thought you liked hanging out with me.'

'We do.' They said together.

'But we've been secretly training you up.'

Shane was confused. 'Keep what secret? What invitation? I don't get it.' His eyes were drawn to the doorway, where his grandfather appeared, grinning.

'Brace yourself, Shaney. Your life's about to change forever.' The old man led him up a narrow flight of stairs to the top floor. There were five stories to this enormous building and around fifteen bedrooms. Brett Splatter skipped along the corridor, tapping the doors, playfully.

'What's going on, grandad? What's all this about a secret invitation?'

The spritely old man eventually stopped, unlocking the final door to the left. 'This is my treasure room. Prepare to be amazed.'

Shane was confused. All he could see as he wandered in was junk. Old paintings, rusty bicycles, creepy looking dolls, musty smelling clothes, you get the picture. 'Is all this for a boot sale?' he asked, following his grandfather to an old, crusty fireplace leaned against the wall.

'This…' Brett Splatter announced, spreading his arms wide, '…is my special collection of goodies from 'Measure the Treasure'.'

Unimpressed, Shane scanned the room and spotted a stained toilet in the corner. 'What, even that rank looking bog?'

'That particular piece,' the old man straightened his tie, 'is called a throne, because the lady who sat on it was a famous Queen.'

'Elizabeth the Second?' said Shane.

'No,' said the bald man, 'Queen Linda of Somewheriun.'

Shane pulled a face. 'Load of old rubbish if you ask me.'

'This is where you are wrong. You see Shaney, one man's rubbish is another man's treasure. Looks can be deceiving.' The old man pointed to some cracked ornaments and broken toys sitting gloomily on the fireplace shelf. 'Do you see anything interesting on here?' he asked. Shane shook his head. 'What about this kids' tractor? Why do I have it? Why is it here?'

Shane yawned. 'I don't care.'

'Well,' his grandfather continued, 'if I lift this little yellow digger up, like this....'

'You're so cringe.'

'...something fascinating happens.'

Shane blew out a sigh and turned away. He was about to walk out when something in his brain told him to turn around. Usually he ignored his brain, but it kept prodding at his eyes and so, with another heavy sigh, he looked back. 'Whoa.' He thought. 'That is pretty fasci-mating.' Part of the wall, the bit with the fireplace, had moved outwards at an angle. His grandfather had just opened a secret door! And now the old man was standing proudly in front of the gap.

'Come through, young Shaney. It's time to welcome you to my top-secret den.'

'Have you got a toilet in there, too?' said Shane.

'On the contrary.' grinned his grandfather, tapping the postcard. 'This is where I keep all my information on that particular trophy.' With the press of a light switch, a glass shelf lit up against the back wall revealing a gold cup that looked very much like the Jules Rimet Trophy. 'Ta- daa!' exclaimed the old man. Shane moved in for a closer look. 'I'm afraid this is only a replica.'

'Can I hold it?' said Shane, grinning.

The bald man gave a small nod. After fussing around in a small cupboard, he handed Shane a face mask and told him to put it on. When Shane asked why, he said the den had just been painted and he didn't want his grandson inhaling harmful fumes. Shane sniffed the air. The smell reminded him of a charity shop, not a freshly painted room. Picking up a stone ornament of a lion, the old man then very carefully lifted the trophy, and dropped the lion in its place.

'It's heavy,' said Shane, taking it from his grandfather. 'Make a good weapon.'

Brett Splatter raised an eyebrow, 'You think?'

'It looks like the real thing' he said, studying it. 'What's the difference between this one and the real trophy?'

The old man smiled 'About a billion pounds.'

Chapter 12

Shane was so shocked his mouth went into spasm. 'A B-b-b-bill-ion?!'

Taking the trophy from him, Brett Splatter very carefully placed it back onto the shelf, removing the wooden carving almost at the same time. He then gestured for Shane to remove his mask. 'The real trophy is a lost antique with great history. It's also made of gold. Add that to the mystery of its disappearance and I'd say you could put a billion-pound price tag on it.'

Shane's mouth was still faulty. 'And, er, and, win, I, can, it?'

'You can and you shall win it.' nodded his grandfather. 'Remember all those books we gave you on the World Cup?'

Shane nodded eagerly, but every single book he'd ever been given had been instantly tossed on what he called 'book mountain' in the corner of his room. Needless-to-say, none of them had been read.

'I hope you've absorbed the info. This competition will no doubt test your World Cup knowledge.'

'Easy' said Shane, relieved that his mouth was working again. 'But I've got a few questions. How do you know this trophy is still around and not rotting under the ocean?'

'Because I've made contact with the woman who has it.'

Shane's eyebrows lifted. 'And how did you know this competition thing was coming?'

His grandfather thought for a moment. 'I gave her the idea. I am a game show host, after all!'

Shane frowned. 'If you know who she is, why don't you just take it from her?'

'Because I can't find her!' the old man cried, suddenly losing his temper. 'Sorry.' He hauled in a few deep, calming breaths. 'It's a delicate matter. I've been looking for that woman and the trophy for over forty years.' He mopped his brow. 'This story goes back a long way. Where do I start?' He paused, thinking. 'Ok, imagine there are two families. It's the 1960s, and one family has just been given a very valuable gold vase.'

'The World Cup?'

'Ok, yes. And this family are poor. Now, the newspapers were saying that the trophy had been stolen.'

'Had it?'

Brett Splatter played with his tie. 'It might have. Anyway, this family had it in their house, and the son loved it so much it slept next to him each night. But one day, the father came home and told the family he was going to sell it.'

'To the second family?'

'No. They haven't entered the story, yet. Dad told us, I mean, the dad told the family that the buyer wore sunglasses and a cap because he didn't want to be spotted by the police.'

'A baddie?'

'Possibly. So, they agreed to a secret place where Mr. Sunglasses would pick up the trophy and drop off a bag full of cash. This drop off point was to be under a special holly bush in the local park.'

Shane looked confused. 'Why couldn't he just go to their house?'

'Because he didn't want to.'

'Why not?

The old man looked irritated. 'Just listen to the story! So, the day came, and the family wrapped the trophy in newspaper and strode off to the park. It was a gorgeous sunny morning, and they were excited because their lives were about to change forever. The son was a bit sad, though, because he loved that cup. The mum and kids played on the swings as dad waited for a moment to place it under the holly bush. With a thumbs up and a whistle signaling to us that he'd dropped it off, they scurried up a nearby tree to hide among the branches and waited for Mr. Sunglasses.'

'Did he come?'

'Well, they waited, and waited. Lunchtime came and the park got busy. Their legs went numb from being stuck in the same position for ages. Then, a kid from the other family came along on his roller skates.

'Finally, the other family arrive.'

'Quiet! This child, he was only ten, stopped by the holly bush, bent down, picked up the parcel and skated off with it, just like that.'

'What did the poor family do?'

'They fell out of the tree because their legs had gone to sleep!'

Shane didn't know whether to laugh or be cross. 'Are we one of those families?' Brett Splatter nodded. 'The roller skating one, right?' The bald man shook his head, slowly. 'We're the losers?!' said Shane, outraged. 'We lost the World Cup to roller skate boy! What happened to him?'

Brett Splatter's face brightened. 'As he was leaving the park, he tripped over a paving slab on his skates and knocked himself out. The parcel went skidding under a car and a dog found it. The mutt's owner called the police, and the trophy was returned to the F.A.'

Shane thought for a moment. 'So, if we're the poor, falling out of tree family, who's the roller skate family?'

The old man gave his grandson a hard stare. 'Let's just say, if James Eligus has been invited to this competition, don't you dare start without me.'

'But when does the woman come into it?' said Shane.

'About twenty years later. I was about to get my trophy back. I went all the way to Brazil. They said I could have it for a small fee. But that cowardly woman stole it from me!' His grandfather rambled on, but Shane's mind had sloped off, wondering what life was going to be like in the billionaire's boys club.

Chapter 13

Shane was the first into the classroom. He had a lot to show off today. This was his chance to prove he was a true winner. This was his chance to show everybody how truly rich and powerful he was about to become. Mr Smith almost fainted when he saw him at the front of the queue.

'I never thought I'd see the day. Shane, is that you? Or are you a hologram?'

The giant boy bounced to his table of four at the back of the classroom and sat down next to Omar with an unusually cheery sigh. Today was going to be awesome. Gold. Money. Winner! With a loud cough he tossed the postcard onto Omar's desk and sat back in his chair, playing it cool. The back legs creaked.

'What's this, Shane?' said Omar, picking it up.

'Just a postcard' he shrugged.

'From your Nan?'

Shane frowned. 'Why would it be from my nan?'

'Nans and grandads are the only people who send postcards. Everyone else sends texts.'

'Yeah, well this is different. This thing invites me...'

'To your Nan's birthday?'

'Stop talking about NANS!' barked Shane. 'I've been invited to a special competition. Top secret. To win the

World Cup. The first one, what England won. And it's made of pure gold!'

Omar took a closer look at the image, scratching the surface with a finger. 'Not real gold though, is it? Probably only gold leaf. You can buy that in Lidl. I love their cheese twists.'

Shane punched Omar on the arm. 'Not the postcard, you doughnut. The real thing. I'm gonna win the real trophy. Then I'm gonna sell it and I'm gonna be rich and I'm gonna flatten this place, so I'll never have to see you idiots ever again.'

Margot sat down, picked up the card and read the back. 'It says to tell no-one. You've just told us two. You might be disqualified.'

'What?! No, I won't.'

'Also, that trophy's been missing for decades' said Margot. 'It was stolen in 1983 in Brazil. Most people think the robbers melted it down for gold.'

'Shut up' said Shane. 'My Grandad says it's still alive. He's got a replica.'

'Maybe it's just a big game that he's made up for you' said Omar.

Shane stood up and thumped his fists down on the table. 'NO, IT'S NOT!' He snatched his postcard and slumped down onto his chair with such force that the back legs snapped, causing him to momentarily disappear.

Chapter 14

James hurried to his seat next to Margot as Shane peeled himself off the floor.

'This chair's bust' he said and sloped off to the front to find a new one. Margot smiled sheepishly at James. 'You ok?' she said, softly.

'Yep' he replied, fussing with his pencil case, unable to meet her gaze.

'Did you go to hospital?'

'No.'

Omar leaned forward. 'Are you really allergic to football?' His fingers shot up to his ears causing Omar to point excitedly. 'Yey, FA Cup!'

'Leave him alone' said Margot.

'I can fight my own battles, alright?' snapped James. 'Just leave me alone.' With a loud tut, he buried his head under his polo t-shirt and rested his head on his folded arms. An awkward silence fell across the table. That is, until Shane returned with a chair he'd stolen from Banksy.

'Why is everyone so quiet?' His little piggy eyes darted across the table for answers until they settled on James' green top. Chuckling to himself, he placed the postcard on the small boy's desk and gripped his shoulders. James froze.

'Little turtle' said Shane, invitingly. 'Little turtle, pop

your head out. There's a lettuce leaf on your desk.'

Slowly, James raised his head but kept his eyes shut tight. This was what he'd been most fearful of all along. This was the reason he'd sworn Margot to secrecy. 'Is it something to do with fleurbler?' he asked.

'No' Shane lied. 'It's something from history, isn't it, Margot!' She agreed, reluctantly. 'See.'

James took a deep breath and gently opened one eye. If the object had anything to do with fleurbler he'd shout for Mr Smith in his loudest voice. But, to his astonishment, he found himself squinting at a familiar shape. He opened the other eye, and the shape was given detail. Detail that made him sit bolt upright.

'Know what that is?' said Shane, taken aback. The small boy nodded. Shane gasped. James flipped over the postcard over and read:

'Dear Shane,
Congratulations! You have been invited to compete in a top-secret competition for the long lost and extremely valuable JULES RIMET TROPHY.

Your first task is to go to www.freejulie.fleb and follow the instructions. You have until 6pm.
Tell no-one else!

Good Luck.'

'Did you get this last night?' asked James.

Shane frowned. 'This morning, with my breakfast. But why aren't you freaking out and crying 'Fleurbler'?!'

James looked confused. 'Why would I do that?'

'Ha!' roared Shane. 'You don't know?'

James shrugged. Margot looked away.

Shane grabbed the postcard and pointed at it. 'That's the football World Cup.' he spat, emphasising the word 'football'. James retreated into his school shirt. 'The biggest thing in the whole of football. Anyone who loves football dreams of winning it!' He stopped, as though he'd been tapped on the shoulder by a disturbing thought. 'Wait a minute. Why did you ask if I got this last night?' James removed a finger from his ear and pointed to his rucksack. Shane wasted no time and tipped it upside down, finding an identical postcard to his. 'You got one too?' James nodded under his top. 'I'm playing against you?!'

'I'm not playing' mumbled James.

As the reality slowly sunk in, Shane's face went from a frown to a smile to a halogen beam. 'My competition is you? YOU?! The kid that's too scared to even say the word 'FOOTBALL'?! I can't lose. I'm gonna be rich. There's nothing stopping me.' He jumped onto the desk and threw his hands out.

'I'M GONNA BE A BILLIONAIRE FOR REAL. AND THEN I'M GONNA BUY THIS SCHOOL AND FLATTEN IT AND MAKE A FOOTBALL GROUND AND A THEME PARK AND THE BIGGEST GO-CART

TRACK IN THE WORLD. AND NONE OF YOU WILL BE ALLOWED IN!'

The class stared silently at him. Shane fiddled with his collar.

'ALRIGHT, SOME OF YOU WILL BE ALLOWED IN. BUT ONLY THE COOL ONES.' He shrugged. 'I DON'T CARE. I'M GONNA BE RICH!'

He got down and returned to his seat. The rest of the class chatted amongst themselves. He looked at James, who popped his head from his t-shirt. A sudden recollection hit him. The two families. Mr Sunglasses. Falling out of trees. Roller skates. Was James a member of the roller skate family? A cunning grin spread from the huge boy's face. Of course he was, the bully decided.

'Oi, Fleurbler.' James looked up, sheepishly. 'I want you to do this challenge against me.' James shook his head. 'I can't play against myself. I need an opponent.'

'No' said James.

'The library, 12.30. Be there. We're gonna start the competition. I wanna see your head explode. And don't even think about running home sick.'

Chapter 15

Morning break came, and James hopped onto his favourite bit of wall feeling queasy. His head was full of questions; Why had Margot betrayed him? And why was she being nice, but then silent? That just made it worse because now all he wanted to do was make up and be friends again. But he couldn't possibly do that because that would show him as being weak, and that trust wasn't important, which it was.

But right now, he could really do with her support and advice. Shane's words were ringing in his ears. 'The library, 12.30. We're gonna start the competition. I wanna see your head explode. And don't even think about running home sick'. He shut his eyes tightly, then became aware that someone had hopped up next to him. The smell of flowers and cucumber wafted up his nostrils. It was Margot, the betrayer. 'What do you want?'

'To say I'm sorry.'

'Pardon?'

Margot pinched one of her ear lobes. Realising he was still in silent mode he lowered his hands. She smiled and repeated her apology.

'Well, now you've said it. Goodbye.'

Being this cold felt rubbish, he thought. But also, good.

She was paying for betraying. He twisted his body away, but she didn't leave. She didn't get the hint. She just sat there, silently, looking ahead, making things even more awkward. He held her silence for a short while but soon cracked under the pressure.

'What else do you want?'

She looked at him and watched him wince and do his FA Cup ears thing when he heard a cheer from the field. She watched him scratch the growing red ring across his forehead, usually hidden by a mass of black curls.

'Do you need any help with Shane and the competition?'

'No.'

'Right, then.' And she jumped down and ran off towards the playing field.

'Was that it?' he wondered. Was she truly sorry or just faking it? He started to feel cheated, let down. Then again, he pondered, he could have just said 'Yes, I need help.' Then they could have talked about why he, a boy allergic to fleurbler, had been invited to win a fleubler cup? Oh, the irony. He could have asked her to be his eyes and ears in the library when this dreaded thing started. And, whether it would it be better to get beaten up by Shane rather than face a fatal allergic reaction from being forced into the competition? Also, why had Shane mentioned grandad Ron? Where was his allergy letter? And why did no-one believe he was allergic to fleurbler?

Too late to ask those questions now. And he didn't ask them throughout History or English either. He didn't say anything for two whole lessons and realised that your throat can feel just as sore when you stay silent as it can when you scream and shout.

At lunchtime, he sat in his usual seat on the Year One table in the far corner by the big window, guzzling water and nibbling on a marmite sandwich. A Year One girl went up to him and asked whether his allergy was real. When he nodded, she stood on the table and shouted, 'It's true everyone, he really thinks he's allergic to football!!!'

Just as the laughter was dying down, he spotted Shane stride into the hall flanked by the Buzzcut brothers. Their eyes scoured the room menacingly. In a flash, James hid under the table and kneeled on a bit of jam sandwich. He popped his head above the table, and through a gap between a shoulder and a sticky-out ear, he caught sight of the boys prowling between the long rows of chattering kids. The only entrance was through a set of doors on the opposite side of the hall. Waiting until the hunters had reached the centre of the centre table, James sprung up and ran for it.

'There he is, Shane!' said blonde Buzzcut.

'Come here, FA Cup!'

Weaving past Miss Buckwell, jinking past a girl with a steaming bowl of apple crumble, James scurried along the perimeter of the excited, echoey hall and made it to the doors just before Shane. Spinning left, he sprinted along the yellow bricked corridor, his feet squeaking on the wooden floor, past his classroom door, past the long collage illustrating why St Mark's was such a great school, past Mr Smith who was just coming out of the toilet.

'James? Shane?' He called, surprised.

'Fleurbler!' puffed Shane.

Taking the final door on the right, James hurried through the reception area where Mrs Landers stood up in alarm. He'd done it. He was going to be free. Though the glass doors he could see the outside world in all its sunny splendour. He pushed the horizontal bar to open the door. This was it. He wasn't going to take part in a stupid deathly competition. He wasn't going to be bullied into anything he didn't want to do. He was running for the hills, and it felt great.

Only the door wouldn't open. He peeked over his shoulder. Still alone except for Mrs Landers, but Shane was coming for him, and Mr Smith too by the sounds of it. He tried again, rattling the bar, pushing as hard as he could.

'Stupid door! What's going on?'

'You can't exit without pressing the button on your left' said Mrs Landers.

Before he could say or do anything, Shane and Mr Smith bundled into the room, both slightly out of breath. He tried one more time, rattle, rattle. Still no joy. Now, Shane was striding up to him. He squeezed his eyes shut and covered his face in defence. But instead of hitting him, Shane tapped him on the shoulder and beamed.

'You're it.'

'Sorry?' said James, completely baffled.

'You know you can't leave the school premises without adult supervision' said Mrs Landers.

'Not trying to escape, were you, James?' said Mr Smith. 'My classes aren't that bad, are they?'

'He takes tag very seriously, sir' said Shane, popping an arm around the shaking boy and giving him a playful squeeze.

'Well, keep it to the playing field' said Mr Smith, ushering them out of the room. 'Don't extend your games to these areas. We're lucky to have all this space. Now, off you go.'

'Yes, sir.' said Shane, keeping a firm grip on James' shoulder and leading him back along the corridor.

Chapter 16

'Can you loosen your grip a bit? My armpit's sore,' said James, breathlessly.

The small boy's feet were scampering at double speed trying to keep up, as Shane led him with a vice like grip, across the playground towards the library.

'You're not squirming out of this one.'

As the building drew ever nearer, James started to really panic.

'Ok, you win.' He sighed, trying to wriggle free. 'The trophy's yours, Shane. I don't want to play!' But the boy giant didn't even flicker. Flailing children bounced off him as the human bulldozer made an arrow-straight route across the playground. James tried a different approach.

'Ok, if you force me to do this, you know I might die. And then you'll go to prison. For years.'

This time, Shane did flicker.

'No, I won't' he said. 'They'll let me off 'cos you're a sad little loser. In fact, they'll thank me and give me a massive medal!' He bundled James down a small set of stairs to the paved area outside and grabbed a wrist. 'It's not my fault you're allergic to football.'

Just then, Margot appeared from nowhere and barged in between them. James bounced against the door. She stuck her chin out at Shane, fearlessly.

'I need to be there to help him.'

Shane shook his head. 'No way.' He lunged for his victim but once again Margot got in between them.

'It's just for safety. If he gets ill, I can call for help. I can also read out the instructions if you like. I mean, I know you don't like reading.'

Shane thought about this and gave a small nod. 'Sounds fair.'

'No!' said James.

Margot and Shane gawped at each other, startled. 'What?!'

'I can do this on my own!'

'But she can read all the words for us' said Shane.

'I don't care. She broke her promise. Now everyone's laughing at me.'

Margot rounded on James. 'I had no choice! I thought you were dying, and I needed their help!'

James looked away. 'You could have told them not to tell everyone.'

Margot looked up to the sky. 'I did! But Omar blurted it to...'

Shane butted in. 'Come on, let's get on with this thing.' And with a swing of the door, and a shove in the back, James found himself heading for the arena of the first challenge.

Chapter 17

On any other day, the library was his favourite place, mainly because James was pretty much guaranteed not to hear any mention of fleurbler. But today, the vibes were completely different. As he made his way, knees knocking, past the musty smelling rows of books towards the bright carpeted area facing the computers, he felt like he was on a boat. He could swear the floor was moving. In a cold sweat, he stumbled to one of the bookcases, stuffed his fingers in his ears and rested his forehead against a row of soothing cool book spines. Shane gave him a little shove on his way past to shut the blinds of the big window. With the room now much darker, Margot's face lit up as she switched on one of the computers and entered the competition website. Shane joined her, insisting on squatting on the edge of his chair like one of the All Blacks doing the Haka. After a short while, these words appeared on the screen:

'FINDJULIE.FLEB, happily the least visited website in the world. Press ENTER to continue'.

The registration process went smoothly for Shane, mainly because Margot filled in all his details. But for James, it was a bit more complicated. For the first few questions she had to run over to him, pull his fingers out of his ears, re-assure him that her question wasn't to do with fleurbler, 'no, honestly James, I just need your date of birth', then rush back to the computer and type his answer. After about question four she got bored with doing that, so she hooked her hand round the crook of his elbow and dragged him closer to the computer, where she shouted the questions at him. With all the boring stuff completed, Margot pushed the ENTER button and waited with Shane, who had put his fingers in his ears to drown out her shouts. True to form, James rushed back to the bookshelf and assumed his regular pose.

For a few moments, the computer screen remained blank, then a simple melody from the speakers cut the silence. The black screen opened into an image of the great footballer, Pele, in his famous Brazil jersey, holding aloft the Jules Rimet Trophy. A title appeared in shiny gold and was accompanied by a voice-over from a lady with a very silky tone.

'Welcome to the great Lost Trophy Challenge.'

First, let's see some of the great work we've achieved with our charity foundation over the years.

Margot and Shane watched a series of clips showing 4G football pitches being laid across dusty plains; changing rooms built, goalposts put up and young children from across the globe enjoying football. A map of the world appeared, and dozens of little red pins dropped across Africa, South America and Asia.

This is where we have built our kids' soccer centres, among some of the poorest communities in the world. We have over a thousand now.

The map was pushed aside to reveal a revolving image of the gleaming Jules Rimet Trophy.

All this from just one little gold cup and some very generous donors.

The image dissolved to show a faded photo of the old World Cup covered with cobwebs sat in a dusty cabinet.

It used to live here, in the basement of the Brazil football headquarters, where no-one could see it. But, on 21 December 1983, it was rescued by a very brave lady who used its beauty and prestige to help those most in need.

Shane rolled his eyes. 'Do-gooders. So lame!'

There is one condition to winning the trophy: We shall expect you to continue this charity work once you take over.

Shane chuckled to himself. 'Fat chance of that. I'm selling it!'

The Lost Trophy Challenge Roundup…

Just like the beginning of Match of the Day, the introduction showed loads of action from various match days, only this time all the goals scored and saved were by kids playing in regular parks.

The voice-over continued.

'In Germany, nine-year-old Fredericka Bertholtz was first on the leader board when she scored an impressive overall twenty-three points. Here's her great attempt at Mario Goetze's 2016 World Cup winner against Argentina. What a goal! Next, we headed to Italy as Emilio Castalli won his tie with twenty-four points. His fantastic Marco Tardelli inspired goal and arm-popping celebration made us all feel like we were back in Spain, 1982. And what about this: a fabulous, drilled shot inside the near-post as twelve-year-old Jorge Suarez did it just like Schiaffino in the 1950 final as Uruguay claimed their second title and gave Jorge twenty-three points. Now, take a look at this right footed screamer; Manuella Do Prado doing a perfect Roberto Carlos from the 1970 World Cup final for Brazil. What a finish! She is the current leader with twenty-five points. There's only one place left to visit now, and that's England. So, without further ado, let's get this final challenge underway.'

Margot paused the action and dragged James closer to the screen, dumping him on the floor by her feet. Impressively, he managed to keep his fingers in his ears and his eyes shut throughout, so he missed the montage of great World Cup goals and the following information from the narrator.

'You will compete in four tasks over the next two weeks. The first round will be a quiz, starting in a moment. One point will be awarded for each correct answer. The remaining tasks will be revealed in due course. The child with the most points at the end will be the victor for their country. If either player scores more than twenty-five points you will be the champion and you will win the Jules Rimet trophy. If players are tied on twenty five points or more, a penalty shootout will decide the winner.'

'Easy!' said Shane, giving James a little kick. 'You look a bit pale, mate.'

'Pardon?' said James, looking up at him, innocently. 'Has it finished? Have you won? Can I go now?'

'I've had enough of this.' the boy giant said, and in a swift move he leaned down and yanked James' hands from his ears. 'If you so much touch those ears for the next hour, I'll rip them off and make you eat them!'

The voice-over lady broke the uncomfortable silence.

'You have been invited to the greatest ever secret treasure competition the world has ever known. We must remind you once again never to tell a soul.'

Margot and Shane shared a guilty look.

'Your questions are based on England's 1966 triumph and the near misses from World Cups and Euro tournaments thereafter.'

A big green button with the word **CONTINUE** flashed brightly in the centre of the screen.

'Once you press this button the game starts, and you will not be allowed to exit. So, one point for each answer. Press that button and let's play!'

Chapter 18

Quick as a flash, Shane leapt across Margot's outstretched palms and pressed it.

'No going back now, FA Cup!'

James shuffled nervously, his back facing the monitor. Voice-over woman continued:

'Question 1. To Shane first.'

The questions appeared on the screen as he asked them. Shane rubbed his hands in excitement.

'Who scored England's second goal in the 1966 World Cup final? Was it a) Bobby Charlton b) Geoff Hurst or c) Martin Peters?'

'That's easy!' cried Shane, jumping up. 'Geoff Hurst.'

'You sure?' said Margot.

'Definitely. He scored a hat-trick.'

Margot clicked the cursor on (B).

'Yesssss!' cried Shane. 'Now let's watch FA Cup boy's head catch fire!'

Margot ignored him. 'As soon as you start feeling ill, James, just raise one of your hands.' He gave a little thumbs-up as the back of his head nodded.

'And now on to you, James. Who scored England's second goal in the 1966 final? Was it a) Bobby Charlton b) Geoff Hurst or c) Martin Peters?'

He was expecting his stomach to blow up or his head to explode. What actually happened was far odder. A bolt of energy fizzed through his body, causing his arms and legs to fly out to the side. While his face twitched crazily his body danced a little jig and then he shouted out 'BLUBBAWIBBY MRTIN PETRS.'

Margot stared at him, and Shane cracked up laughing.

'I dunno what just happened' said James, shocked.

'I do' said Shane, licking his lips. 'Your body's getting ready to explode. There's gonna be blood everywhere!'

'The correct answer was (c) Martin Peters. Well done, James.'

Shane stared at the screen, stunned. 'But' he stuttered. 'That's not right! This thing's a scam!'

He punched his chair and rubbed his knuckles, sulkily. Margot turned to James.

'Pretty good guess.'

'Yeah.'

His eyes were suddenly drawn to the screen showing the clip of Martin Peters' goal. The ball is hooked into the penalty box by Hurst. It ricochetss off a defender straight into the path of Peters, who stabs the ball home from six yards.

'I've seen this before!' he cried, kneeling up and pointing with a crooked finger. 'In my nightmare from last night. I mean, dream. I mean…whatever it was.'

'Is your stomach hurting?' said Margot.

He gave it a prod. 'No. This is weird'

'Let's move on to the next question.' said Shane, more cheerfully. 'There's a long way to go!'

'Number 2' announced voice-over lady.

'For Shane first, please. What was the name of the 1966 World Cup mascot?

Was it: A) Bulldog Bobby B) Lenny the Lion, or C) World Cup Willy?'

Shane jumped up, waving a victory fist in the air.

'Easy.' he announced. 'Bulldog Bobby. Have that!' He jabbed a finger at the screen as if it had done something to offend him. Margot entered his answer (A).

'And don't copy me, FA Cup boy!'

James closed his eyes and once again his body went into spasm. He flew to his feet, arms flapping uncontrollably. His head jerked forward, and he strode towards the window walking like an excited chicken. While he was doing this, a distant memory fizzed into life.

He was in a small square room with a big desk and two computer screens. Blurred neon signs hung over three of the walls. Splashed across another was a big map of the world with red pins dotted around it. A wrinkled, suntanned hand gave him a tatty soft toy lion wearing a Union Jack top.

He stopped, dead centre, facing away from the screen, and after a few more jerks of the head, he said 'SIBALANANA WORLD CUP WILLY'.

'That's well wrong!' cried Shane jumping from his seat.

James squinted, took a deep breath and turned around. 'Did I say World Cup Willy?'

Margot nodded. 'Aye. Let's see who's right, eh?'

'Well, it ain't gonna be him,' said Shane.

'The correct answer is (C) WORLD CUP WILLY. Well done again, James. That puts you 2-0 two-nil up.'

Chapter 19

No-one could quite believe what was happening. Shane ran over to a bookshelf and punched it, while James shuffled close to Margot. Not too close, though. He still hadn't entirely forgiven her.

'I had a kind of weird vision, just then. That's how I knew the answer. I don't know if it was a memory or just made up. It's so strange, Margot.'

She nodded, sympathetically, and reached out to touch his neck. At first, he moved away.

'I just want to check your glands. Make sure they're not swollen. Have you got any skin rashes? Is your mouth closing up? These are all allergy signs. I looked it up online after you told me your secret.'

James leaned in to let her check. Maybe she wasn't such a bad friend, after all.

'All fine' said Margot. 'Maybe you're not as allergic as you thought you were.'

He gave her a gentle nod, and said they should continue with another question, see if it brought up some other visions or memories. Shane returned breathlessly to his seat, his face blotchy and his knuckles red raw.

'Next question.' he demanded. 'Bring it, allergy boy!'

'**Question 3**' announced the voice-over lady. This time, all three children leaned forward in anticipation.

'**Who was the 1966 tournament's highest goal scorer: a) Geoff Hurst of England b) Eusebio of Portugal or c) Helmut Haller of West Germany? James, why don't you go first this time.**'

Shane threw his hands in the air. 'Why are they all about 1966? It was a million years ago!'

James closed his eyes. This time there were no chicken impressions or crazy arm movements. He just suddenly felt tired and curled up in a ball on the floor. Within moments, a dormant, cobwebbed section of his brain lit up.

He was in his garden, playing football with his dad, who was demonstrating very badly how to do overhead 'scissor' kicks. 'It wasn't only Pele who did these' he said, launching into another failed attempt and landing awkwardly on his back as the ball dropped onto his stomach. He got to his feet, giggling. 'Eusebio, top scorer in 1966, was a master at the overhead, too!'

James opened his eyes, feeling strangely refreshed, like he'd had a brilliant night's sleep.

'It's Eusebio' he said, emphatically, turning to Shane, 'and no copying me this time.'

Shane looked like he was going to internally combust. He looked befuddled, flustered, flummoxed and furious.

'Copy YOU? YOU?' he bellowed, sending an innocent chair flying across the floor. 'Hurst. Geoff Hurst for England with fifteen goals!'

'The correct answer is (b) Eusebio of Portugal. He scored nine goals helping his team to the semi-finals. Well done James. That makes the score three-nil to you.'

'AAAAAARRRGGGHGHGGHGGHG!!!!!' screamed Shane. This was about as much as he could take. His face, now a patchy purple, was screwed up like a crisp packet. He paced around the room like a caged tiger grabbing at his wiry hair.

'Do you wanna stop, Shane?' asked Margot, with just a hint of sarcasm.

'NOOOO!!!!!'

Chapter 20

And so, it continued.

Each question was answered correctly by James and incorrectly by Shane, who took to punching the carpet lots. With each question, James was rewarded with a fresh memory of his dad or grandad. What concerned him more than anything, was that all these new memories - surely, they were memories because they contained his family - were all connected to Fleurbler. So surely, if he was allergic to the sport, he should technically be dead by now. So why wasn't he? Also, how did he know all these things about the 1966 World Cup? It was so obscure. And why was he suddenly feeling stronger than he'd ever felt, as though these fresh memories were giving him huge power boosts? All James knew was that he didn't want the questions to stop.

'What was the name of the dog who found the trophy after it was stolen?'

'Grandad talked about him. It was Pickles,' said James.

'Rover,' said Shane.

'Correct James.'

'How many goals did Pele score in the 1966 finals?'

'I read about this, in a big red book. Did he get injured

against someone early on?' Margot gazed at James in amazement. 'Yes, against Portugal, and he only got one goal,'

'Five!' said Shane.

'Correct James.'

There was a brief glimmer of hope for Shane when the more modern questions were asked, such as:

'Who scored England's only goal in the 2018 World Cup semi-final against Croatia? Was it a) Harry Kane: b) John Stones or c) Kieran Trippier?'

'C! Roared Shane. 'Trippier with a free kick!'

'Correct Shane!'

'Who scored the first goal in the 2021 Euro final at Wembley?'

'Luke Shaw'

'Well done, Shane. Another point for you. Who won the golden boot at the 1990 tournament? a) Gary Lineker: b) John Barnes or c) Paul Gascoigne. James first please.'

He didn't know the answer. His brain was so overheated what with all these rekindled old memories popping back into the scene that he threw his hands out and guessed.

'Lineker?'

Shane burst out laughing. 'Lineker does Match of the Day and crisp adverts. It's Gazza, you radish!'

'It's Gary Lineker, I'm afraid Shane. James wins the point.'

Eventually, they reached the final question. James was

now stood behind Margot, while Shane had replaced him on the floor, curled up in a squishy ball of frustration.

'Who was England's World Cup winning captain?'

'Was it a) Nobby Stiles b) Jack Charlton or c) Bobby Moore? Shane first, please.'

Shane lifted his head slightly and with an utterly deflated crimson croak, answered 'Bobby Moore'. James nodded his agreement.

'The correct answer is indeed Bobby Moore.'

James grinned, nervously. Although he'd gone through ten football related questions without dying, there was that nagging feeling in the back of his mind that a hideous killer lurching pain in his stomach was just around the corner; that he was playing with a small fire that was about to engulf him. There was no way he could celebrate yet.

'Well done gentlemen. However, there can be only one winner, and today, it is James. The final score after round one is:

Shane 4 – James 6.'

Shane clambered onto his hands and knees and slowly rose like a defeated Godzilla from the ocean. Shrugging off his disappointment, he fixed James with a defiant glare.

'You're not allergic to football. You fixed this. You're just a skinny little liar!'

James stared back. 'I'm not, I promise.'

To their surprise, Shane then kicked off both his trainers and removed his black Man Utd socks, The diabolical smell coming from his feet brought tears to their eyes.

'They're disgusting.' James cried, turning away. 'What are you doing?'

'I'm gonna prove it.' The smell suddenly got a whole lot worse as Shane rubbed his socks in the small boy's face. 'See? You're not dying. You answered all those questions and never died, never even got an itch. You're about as allergic to football as I am burgers. You're a fake. But I'm gonna make sure I win the rest of these challenges. You think you can play dirty? You don't know the meaning of the word. I'm gonna be filthy!' With that, he picked up his trainers and stormed out.

'His feet are filthy' said James rubbing his face with his top.

Chapter 21

'CONGRATULATIONS JAMES!' said the voice-over lady. A fanfare blared from the speakers.

'As a little treat, we're going to show you all the highlights from that wonderful final. You will receive details of your next task shortly. Congratulations once again on a sterling start to this competition!'

Voice-over lady signed off as England, in red shirts, and West Germany in white shirts and black shorts emerged from the tunnel at Wembley stadium to raucous cheers and waving flags. Hurst and Peters kicked off for England and before they knew it England's defence were being tested. Haller thundered in a shot from outside the box that Gordon Banks, England's goalkeeper did well to hold onto. But then, Germany scored.

Margot glanced over at James, but his eyes were fixed, trance-like to the screen. He was what adults call 'miles away'. A memory had sparked - in full glorious colour.

He was back at home, curled up on the sofa, clutching his battered World Cup Willie cuddly toy, watching this very match with his dad. He could smell his father's aftershave, feel the warmth of his arms and gaze up into his blue eyes.

'Look how quick Bobby Moore gets up after being fouled,' James heard his dad saying, pointing to the TV. 'He looks

up, the Germans are still organising their defence as Bobby Moore floats in a beauty straight to Geoff Hurst and…Bang! A glorious glancing header. One-one. We're back in it!'

James continued to hear his father's voice commenting on the match as he watched the highlights, oblivious to the tears that rolled down his cheeks. The match was almost over. England were leading 3-2. In a desperate effort to even the score, West Germany had thrown everyone up the field. However, their last attack had amounted to nothing and Bobby Moore, cool as a cucumber, chested the ball down and hit a sixty yard pass forward to the onrushing Geoff Hurst.

'There's some people on the pitch. They think it's all over…' cried the commentator.

'Watch this for a finish.' grinned dad, taking his tiny hand and clasping it gently. Hurst, with Alan Ball screaming for it over by the right flank, pushed the ball forward with one touch before belting it from the edge of the box into the top right corner of the goal.

'…it is now!' gasped the commentator. Dad threw James up in the air and held him tight. The final whistle blew, and the crowd went crazy. The West Germans fell to the floor in despair. Some England players were in tears, others embraced, and James realised his dad had left the room. As Bobby Moore led his victorious team up the steps James felt his father's presence once more.

He was dressed all in black. And there was a big holdall on the floor with lots of tools and torches inside.

'*Where are you going, daddy?*' *he asked. His father pointed once more to the TV, where Bobby Moore was shaking hands with the Queen. The England captain received the trophy with a bow, turned to the cheering supporters and held it high above his head for all the world to see.*

'*I'm going to rescue that trophy.*' *said dad.* '*It's my duty, and it'll be yours one day.*'

'*Daddy!*' James shouted, but the memory softly faded away. He emerged from his trance to find tears streaming down his face as the 1966 England team paraded the Jules Rimet trophy around a delirious Wembley. He turned to Margot, wiping his tears away.

'It's all coming back to me' he sniffed. 'Dad said he said he was going to rescue the Jules Rimet Trophy. If that's true, I don't understand why he was arrested for stealing jewellery.' He scratched his head, bemused. 'Also, Shane's right. How could I know all those questions if I'm allergic to fleurbler?'

'But you have a letter from the doctor. I've seen it.'

James shrugged. 'Maybe it's a fake?'

'Really?'

He switched off the computer while Margot pulled open the blinds. Sunlight streamed into the room as they walked across the room.

'Will you come to the doctors with me?' said James, opening the door.

'To check your allergy?' said Margot.

'No, to see if Dr Percival works there.'

Chapter 22

The doctors' surgery was hot and smelt of old jumpers. A handful of patients were sitting on hard chairs in the stuffy waiting area while the receptionist chewed gum and tapped away at her computer. As James and Margot walked in, a loud buzzer rang out making them both jump.

'MRS AMPADO!' shouted the receptionist, and an old lady shuffled past, coughing loudly. As James scanned the room, he fully expected to remember the place, but not one corner or smell felt familiar to him, which wasn't especially surprising considering huge chunks of his memory were still missing. With a friendly nudge from Margot, he went up to the receptionist's desk and coughed politely to grab her attention. When this didn't work, he squeaked a greeting. When this didn't work, he waved his hands in front of her computer. Finally, she glanced up at him with bored eyes.

'Sign in please.' she said, in between slow chews, and pointed to a touchscreen against the wall.

James shook his head. 'Sorry, I don't think you under…'

'All patients have to sign in to see a doctor.' She went back to tapping and chewing.

'Erm, no.' said James, a little more confidently. 'I just want some information please?'

The young woman flicked her long brown hair and looked him up and down. 'Where's your mum?'

James bowed his head. 'She's...' he pointed to the sky, 'in heaven.'

'Oh' said the young woman, coughing awkwardly. 'Sorry to hear that. You got a dad?' James nodded. 'Where is he?'

'In prison.'

'Blimey.' She puffed out her cheeks. Her face softened. 'So, who looks after you, honey?'

'My auntie Sue.'

'Is she here?'

'No, she doesn't like going out.'

'But you need an adult with you for an appointment.'

'I haven't got an appointment. I just need some information.'

'We don't give out information, honey. Try the internet.' And with a thin smile, she went back to tapping and chewing.

The tension was clearly getting to James because at this point, he shook his head wildly and told her he only wanted to know whether a certain doctor still worked at this practice. His decisiveness seemed to work because she then asked for the doctor's name. How could he possibly ever forget that? He'd looked at his allergy letter every night for the past two years hoping the information might have changed, or he'd mis-read it in some way.

'Dr Percival, you say?' The woman thought for a moment. 'Are you sure you got the right surgery?'

'Yes.'

'Well,' she said with a sigh. 'I can assure you there's no Dr Percival working here, honey.' Tap, tap, chew, chew.

'What about two years ago? That's when the letter was written.'

She explained that she'd only been working there for the last six months.

'Can you check for me? Maybe he was a substitute doctor?'

'A locum you mean?'

James frowned. 'He's not an insect.'

The woman rolled her eyes. 'A locum, not locust. It's the name for a substitute doctor.'

'Oh.'

'Hang on' she said. Tap, tap, chew, chew.

The wait was agonising. James felt his pulse race and his palms go all damp and clammy. Margot tried taking his mind off the result by telling him about the last time she went to the doctor's. Her little brother had stuffed one of his nostrils with blu tack and peanut bu...

'Right, I've looked down a long list of every person who's worked here for the past ten years.'

'Yes?' said James, jumping to attention.

'Right. Yes, well, Dr Percival' she announced almost like a TV host.

'Yes?'

'From your letter.'

'Yes??'

She was pausing, possibly deliberately, and these pauses seemed to go on much longer than any talent show result he'd ever seen on telly.

'Dr Percival...' another long pause, '...has NEVER worked at this surgery. Your letter is a FAKE!

Chapter 23

Brett Splatter was furious with his grandson. He thundered along the corridor towards the games room with a face the same colour as a very cross volcano. Shane was in for it.

The old man stopped for a second by the doorway. The games room was a huge, converted barn with oak beams, a ping-ping table, a giant horseshoe-shaped sofa, a rope swing, crash mats and a pull-down projector screen. His grandson was on the PlayStation, shooting at far away enemies with a giant machine gun. Brett Splatter looked at the back of his grandson's angular head and ground his teeth. He marched up behind the sofa and swiped the headset from Shane's ears with a swift clip. He then snatched the boy's controller and launched it at the projector. The screen went dead with an expensive sounding fizz. Shane cowered.

'What are you doing? I was down to the last five!'

Brett Splatter straightened up. 'You didn't listen to me, you nincompoop!'

'Eh?' There was a dangerous pause. Shane suddenly realised what he'd done. His face went all blotchy.

'You went on the website, didn't you?' Shane looked away.

Brett Splatter grabbed him. 'I've just been on there,

myself. It says James Eligus won the first task 6 -4. What did we discuss only this morning?'

'I forgot.'

'You forgot what, exactly?'

'To tell you about 'Fleurbler' being invited.'

'And?'

'Er, don't start the competition.'

'Exactly. And what did you do?'

Shane sprung to his feet, defensively. 'He said he was allergic to football. I thought it'd be easy!'

Brett Splatter raised a commanding finger. 'Shane, listen to me very carefully. He's dangerous. All the Eligus' are dangerous.'

'No, he's not, he's a tiny weakling that I'm gonna knock into next door.'

'It's next week.'

'What is?'

'The phrase is, knock into 'next week', not 'next door'. He's not a neighbour.'

'Oh.'

'And you're not going to do that.'

Shane straightened up, defiantly. 'I am!'

'No, Shane, you're not, because if you hurt James in any way, you'll be excluded from the school and thrown out of the competition.'

Shane looked down, glumly.

'But don't worry,' continued the old man. 'There are still a few more tasks, and let's face it, the general knowledge quiz was never going to be your strong point, was it?' Shane shook his head, meekly. 'Here's what's going to happen, you'll take the next few days off school.'

'Eh?'

'Some of the kids might laugh at you for losing a football quiz to a kid who's allergic to football. I want you to watch clips of the most famous World Cup goals and recreate them with Les and Brian. Also, I'm switching off the gaming consoles.'

'What?!'

Brett nodded his head. 'And I'll be watching via the CCTV on my phone. I know you can wrap them round your little finger, but not me. I'm also gonna pay a little visit to a special friend.' The old man rubbed his hands, cunningly.

Shane smirked. 'You sound like you're playing my PlayStation game, grandad.'

'This is more than a game, son' replied Brett. 'This is more serious than life and death.'

Chapter 24

No-one was allowed in auntie Sue's room except auntie Sue. She even had a sign on her door that helpfully pointed out: 'TRESPASSERS WILL GET MASHED UP!!'

As James crept in, the smell of sweaty arm pits hit him like a furnace. How could she sleep in this stench? He put a forearm to his nose and breathed through his mouth. Clothes lay strewn across the room as though they'd been fired from a cannon. Finding his allergy letter among all this mess was like finding a coin in a ball-pit. In the middle of the room was an unmade bed. The walls were covered in faded silver patterned wallpaper which looked like it was trying to escape. As he took it all in, a memory tumbled into his head.

It was Christmas morning. He was in this room, snuggled next to Dad in bed. Wrapping paper and toys were spread across the duvet. A song played on the radio: 'Simply Having a Wonderful Christmas Time' by Paul McCartney. It had been Mum's favourite Christmas song. They shared a hug, looked to the sky, and wished her a Merry Christmas. Dad pulled away and for some reason pointed to the wallpaper behind him and said it needed changing. He explained that Mum had chosen it before their wedding.

James heard a squeak from downstairs. The living room

door had been opened.

'OI!' shouted Auntie Sue.

He crept out to the landing as quietly as possible. He stood at the top of the stairs and peered down. She was at the bottom, looking up.

'Yes?' James quivered, trying to sound cool.

'You only put three sugars in this tea. I always have four!'

He stomped down the stairs, brushed past the laziest woman in the universe, got told off, dolloped more sugar in her tea, brushed past her, got told off again, climbed the stairs and pretended to go into his bedroom. Hearing the living room door slam shut, he peered over the landing bannisters to make sure she'd gone back into the front room. Satisfied, he gently padded back into the murky bedroom of doom and this time, was determined to be quick.

Closing the door behind him, he started his search for the allergy letter by looking under her bed. He crouched down but immediately jumped up again. It smelt of the four F's – foul feet and fried food. Maybe later. Next, was her bedside table drawer, which meant either clambering across the crusty bed or going around it. He decided on the latter, but a creaky floorboard squeaked halfway round so he gave up and wondered if she'd hidden it in the wardrobe. He pulled at the door and the handle fell off. He was back to square one. searching under the murky depths of her bed.

Taking a deep breath, he lowered himself onto all fours, pushed his head into the darkness and very tentatively started feeling around for a letter. Oddly, the first things he came across were a pair of old training shoes, which he thought was strange as Auntie Sue only ever wore those horrible beige slippers. After more fumbling he found some material, sticky, possibly clothing? Between thumb and forefinger, he dragged it out, into the light ...*Eurgh, knickers! HEURGH!?*

He dived back in, wriggling deeper into the depths this time, brushing his hair against the cold bed springs above. With his hands swimming around blindly, he brushed aside yet more seaweed like sticky clothes, but then found a shoe box, and another. He pressed down on the carpet and felt a warm squish on his palm. Stifling a scream, he wriggled out, hooking both shoe boxes with him in the process. A tiny, grey, flattened dead mouse was stuck to his hand. 'AAAAARGH!' he squeaked, stomping his feet in horror, and flicked the poor creature against the wardrobe.

After wiping his hand on her duvet, he bent down to check out the boxes. The first was blue with three stripes running across it. Written in marker pen on the top was the word '**JUBO**.' The other, burgundy in colour, was marked '**JAMES**'. They smelt musty like the doctor's surgery. He pulled the '**JAMES**' box close and flipped the lid open. Sitting on top of a stack of photos, folded in half, was the familiar lettering of his allergy letter.

So, she had taken it. His auntie had stolen from him and lied to him. '*No, I haven't seen it.*' With her stupid, gormless expression. A cauldron of anger rose inside him. He grabbed the letter, scrunched it up into a tight ball and tore at it, shredding the paper into tiny pieces.

In his fury he failed to notice Auntie Sue standing in the doorway.

Chapter 25

'WHAT YOU DOING IN 'ERE?!' she hissed viciously, with arms folded. He froze, unable to speak, as tiny leaves of paper fluttered like snow all around him. 'You read the sign?' She didn't wait for an answer. 'It says 'TRESPASSERS WILL GET MASHED UP!' Now you're in for a mashing!'

He thought of her as a giant potato masher and him a poor, defenceless spud. But wait, this spud had ammunition. He held up the last remaining fragment of the letter, a tiny, screwed up scrap between his fingers, and thrust it towards her like it was Excalibur, the magic sword.

'Why did you take my allergy letter?'

She stood, startled for a moment like a boxer on the ropes. But, like all good fighters, she shook it off and went back on the attack.

'No-one snoops around in my bedroom, in my private property. No-one!' She shuffled towards him and leaned in, pointing a chubby finger just millimetres from his nose.

James quivered like a jelly on a roof and glimpsed into his future. The house would be sold. Auntie Sue would run off up the road skipping and he'd be sent to live with a family of rats on a roundabout.

'You're grounded.' Her voice was low and gravelly as

she dished out his punishment. 'You're not going on the computer unless it's to pay one of my bills. You cook every meal; clean all my clothes and I get a fried breakfast every morning.' She swung her pointy finger towards the door and rocked back on her heels. 'You're just lucky I don't cancel your phone call with your dad this week. Now GET OUT!!'

Chapter 26

It had taken ten minutes for Margot to coax James away from his beloved bit of wall to where they were stood now. It was much cooler today and clouds wandered gloomily across the sky.

'Slowly open your eyes and take your fingers out of your ears' she shouted, above the lunchtime din. With a giant gulp he followed her instruction and found himself at the top of the sloping bank looking down on a game of football. It made him feel dizzy.

'I don't think this is a good idea' he said, instantly squeezing his eyes. 'I mean, what if I'm still allergic?'

'James, you've never been allergic to football. Auntie Sue made it up.' He knew she was right, but for some crazy reason he couldn't quite believe it.

'Let's come back tomorrow. Maybe I'll feel better.' He went to leave but Margot stopped him.

'Look how football has already helped to open up your memory, remembering how you used to watch the World Cup with your dad? You liked football before he went away, now you can learn to like it again.'

James stared at the grass. 'I'd have to do it in secret. Auntie Sue would get rid of me if she caught me.'

Margot grunted. 'Auntie Sue can get lost! This sport

could be the key to completely unlocking your memory, and you might just win a gold trophy along the way.'

Slowly, his eyes moved up until they met hers. Sometimes, he'd noticed, Margot had grey eyes, like a school jumper. They were grey when he'd argued with her before the first task. But right now, they were like a swimming pool blue, encouraging, inviting, warm. He took a deep breath, clenched his jaw, and swung his whole face towards the match. Forcing himself to watch, he looked like a meercat staring at a floodlight. Grass, clouds, trees, houses, kids running. To his relief, he realised he was peering at the same world that he'd always been used to. The only difference was these kids were chasing something round and bouncy.

Margot put a friendly hand on his shoulder. 'Keep watching and keep telling yourself you're not allergic to football.'

He tried the phrase out for size.

'I'm not allergic to…Fleurbler.' As his eyes got used to the excitement and drama of the match, Margot got him to repeat the phrase again and again. James discovered, the more he said it, the more he believed it and the louder he became.

'I'M NOT ALLERGIC TO FLEURBLER!' he cried, spreading his arms out wide. For a moment, he felt incredible. But then, a group of girls who were sat on the bank, started giggling and repeating the word 'fleurbler'. His face started throbbing and he sat down, embarrassed, pulling his knees up to his chin. Margot told them to shut up, but he knew that if he wanted people to stop laughing at him, he'd need to come to terms with a certain unspoken word.

Chapter 27

'Let's break it down,' she said, perching next to him. 'Football.' Two easy little words joined together. So, let's start by saying the word 'foot.'

James twitched.

'Flaaar' he said, like a hissing lizard.

She gave him one of those smiles that said she was in for a tough afternoon's work.

'Ok. Try again, but this time when you're saying it, think of something different, like, a chicken.' James looked confused.

She explained. 'Well, whenever my mum wants me to eat something disgusting, like tuna, she tells me to imagine it's chicken.'

James frowned. 'So, say the word but think of chicken?

'Aye.'

He sighed, 'Alright' and squeezed his eyes shut. After a few moments his brain unveiled a strange image of a giant chicken, who took one ghastly look at a football and passed out.

'Feeeeiiint.' he said, squirming. Margot wasn't impressed. He tried again. This time the chicken was pecking at a scattering of fresh seeds on the grass. 'Feeeeed' he said. She shook her head.

This time he was really going to try and say the word. Just two syllables. Surely it wasn't that difficult. He took a deep breath, pushed his top front teeth down hard on his bottom lip and closed his eyes.

'Fffffffff'.

As he spoke, he imagined another chicken, but this time a surprising little puff of air flew from its rear end.

'Faaaaaart!' he exclaimed.

'Excuse me?'

'Sorry.'

'That'll have to do for now. We haven't much time left. Now try the word 'ball' and imagine this time it's a... potato.'

'Why potato?'

'I don't know. Just try it.'

Once again, his imagination set to work, and he saw a cooked potato being hit with a masher.

'Bashed.'

'Bashed?'

'Yes, like mashed potato.'

'Keep trying.'

'Ok, Boast, like roast.'

'You're not trying, and 'boast' doesn't sound like 'ball' does it?'

'Nah.' he admitted. 'What about boil? Like, boiled potatoes.'

'Fine.' she shrugged. 'So, what have we got? Put the words together.'

'Faaart boil' said James. He could tell she wasn't impressed by the way she looked to the sky and shook her head.

'Whatever.' she sighed. 'Now, try putting it into a sentence.'

Just then, Omar arrived panting. 'What are you up to?' he said.

'Hey Omar,' said James, nudging Margot. 'Wanna go down and play some faaart boil?

Omar shook his head. 'No mate, I'm off to play footy with Banksy. Coming Margot?'

Chapter 28

'Hello son, how are you?'

James always felt a swell of emotion crash into his throat whenever he heard dad's voice, but over the past few months he'd been able to get through the conversation without crying. He'd also noticed that recently, Dad had got into the habit of asking the same set of questions:

1. How's school?
2. Are you looking after your auntie?
3. What records have you been playing?
4. Have you been round to Grandad's old house and picked up his post?

Tonight, was no different. James answered politely, while all the time trying to work out if his dad was happy through the tone in his voice. This was often hard because Dad was good at sounding jolly even when he was sad. But this evening it was James who felt his tone sounded different. He was dying to tell him about the trophy competition, about not being allergic to faartboil, about Auntie Sue making the allergy up. But she was hovering in the background, listening in, making sure none of that was said.

'You sound a bit odd, Jamesy' said dad, after the last question. 'Anything you wanna tell me?'

James glanced at auntie Sue, and after a pause said, 'No. It's ok.'

'Can you put auntie Sue on for a sec?' James passed her the receiver.

'What do you want?' After a few seconds, she tutted, passed the phone back to James and went to look in a sideboard drawer at the far end of the front room.

'Dad?' James said eagerly. He was dying to tell him everything.

'Listen,' said dad, urgently. 'We've only got a few seconds. Auntie Sue tells me you're much better, but she caught you snooping in her room?' James grimaced, preparing for a telling off. 'I dunno what you were looking for,' he continued, 'but you're not gonna find it in her bedroom. And why haven't you gone to Grandad's old house yet to pick up his letters?'

'Because' said James, with a little pause, 'it's just gonna be junk mail. There's no point. And the new people will just tell me to get lost for wasting their time.'

'Please, can you go there tomorrow? I've been asking you for a few months now. It's important.'

James didn't like his dad being cross with him. It hadn't happened very often on the phone but today especially felt like it was spoiling their precious time. It also felt wasteful because James had so much to ask him and now, he'd never get the chance because Auntie Sue was on her way back.

'Yes, I promise I'll do it.'

After they'd said their goodbyes and the receiver was

placed down, Auntie Sue raised a chubby, halting hand.

'Stay where you are.'

James gazed at her, puzzled. She unhooked her left arm from behind her back and handed James a small, framed photograph. Looking at it, he stepped back in shock. Auntie Sue nodded uncomfortably.

'Your dad says you're ready to start opening up your memory. Do you remember your mum?' She pointed to the photo. 'That was taken just after you were born, when you left the hospital.' She shuffled, awkwardly. 'Now listen. I don't want any funny business. No more crying for weeks on end. And if that's what you were looking for in my room then, there you are. But no more snooping around, right? Now, off you go. Measure the Treasure's on in a minute.'

Chapter 29

In the photo, Mum, with her cute button nose and almond shaped eyes, was gazing down lovingly at baby James wrapped up in her arms. Dad was leaning down next to her, his cheek almost touching hers, beaming proudly at the camera.

He hadn't seen her face for such a long time. Auntie Sue had taken all the family photos down after she'd moved in because she thought they would be too painful for James to look at.

She had long shiny black hair. The ends were spiky, and James liked to pinch little tufts together and push them to his skin. He did it all the time now with his own hair, that's why he liked it long. She had the biggest, brownest eyes in the world. She had a big red coat which she used to wrap him inside when picking him up from playgroup. Her smell was sweet and summery, and he loved the softness of her cheeks.

I was in nursery at St Marks. I was drawing with a purple crayon. Don't know why I remember that. Mrs Beeching took me to the office where Dad was waiting with bloodshot eyes. Mum had been run over. She died the next day. The house felt empty. Me and Dad sat at her grave with all the pretty flowers. They were alive and colourful, but my Mum was dead. It didn't seem fair. Dad cried a lot. He said there was no point bottling it up. Better out than in. He said that about doing farts too.

We started going up the motorway to watch...

he paused,

...Faartboil. A team called Luton Town. They played in an orange kit, and I liked it because even though it was cold outside, I felt warm because all these people were sat around me in the stands joking and shouting and cheering. And after a while I remember dad started smiling again. And soon we were celebrating promotion. How do I know these words?

He raced to the window, flung open the curtains and threw up the sash to draw in some fresh air. It was a warm, clear night. He was confused, yet also curious. The connection between Dad and faartboil was there again. Did his father still follow Luton Town? What was the Championship? He gazed up at the scattered stars to think some more when a small silver drone swooped down and faced him.

Chapter 30

It was hovering so close that he could make out every detail; from its pointy beak like nose, the sleek, silver body to the almost silent copter blades whizzing above each wing. It was a truly impressive machine. However, peeking into other people's windows without their permission was wrong, so he told it to go away. It didn't move. He waved his arms at it. 'Go on, get lost!' Still, it stayed. He then said he was going to phone the police. At this point, it gave a little shake of the beak, as if to say 'no'. Then, two little flaps dropped down from its body, and it spat out a paper aeroplane that flew past his ear and landed on his bed.

Picking it up, he smoothed out the folds and saw a photo of the gold Jules Rimet trophy. It was the same picture as his original invitation.

'Did you make up the competition?' he asked the drone. Its beak bowed, slowly. He flipped the card over and quickly scanned over instructions for 'TASK 2'.

'Who are you?' he said and heard a faint scratching noise from inside the machine. After a few seconds, it spat out another paper aeroplane which hit the curtain and landed on the windowsill. This time the card read 'A FAMILY FRIEND.'

He couldn't work it out. The only family he had was

Dad and Auntie Sue. Did they have friends? Possibly, though none had been to the house since Dad went to prison. He looked up to ask the drone a question, but it had disappeared. He pushed his head out the window and peered left and right, scanning back gardens, shed roofs, chimney tops, but it had gone. Slumping down on his bed, he picked up the Jules Rimet card and read the back properly this time.

Dear James,
TASK 2:
To prove your family has a connection with the trophy, please take a World Cup trinket to the venue of this GROUP 1 MATCH from the 1966 FINALS:
FRANCE v URUGUAY
SEAT no: 278 West Stand Upper Tier.
You have until Saturday @ 2pm. Good Luck

He needed a song to help him think. He fingered through his crate of records and plucked a random album out. 'PURE GARAGE ANTHEMS' said the cover. He didn't like the sound of it, so he slid it back and pulled out another: 'HIDEAWAY' a 12' single. He wrinkled his nose and pushed the thin disc back into the stack. Sometimes the record lottery just didn't want to be helpful. Just as well then, that the radio was a good back up.

'Hey, you've got to hide your love away' sang The Beatles,

as James folded the card back into a paper aeroplane.

Prove your family connection to the World Cup? He wondered. The drone must have picked him by mistake because there was no way any of his family had anything to do with something as prestigious as the World Cup. It was too preposterous to even consider. World Cup people owned gold hotels and went to the shops in helicopters. In comparison, Dad was in prison and Auntie Sue lived on benefits. With a shake of the head, he gave the paper aeroplane one last look and sent it flying out of the window, watching it crash land with a flurry of spins on his lawn.

He got ready for bed and took one last look at his new family photo before switching off the light and snuggling under the covers.

Chapter 31

More out of curiosity than anything else, he wanted to see if this match between France and Uruguay had taken place. They were in the hushed library hunched over one of the computers. Rain pattered lightly against the windows. There was no sunlight streaming through the blinds for today, the sun was taking a day off. Having entered the match into the search engine, James was hoping to see an error message or discover they'd only played each other at table tennis or Minecraft or cooking. He didn't even get that far though because the year 1966 flashed up immediately and he felt compelled to click on the link.

'See?!' said Margot pointing at the screen. 'France won 2-1. Click on 'more information." They soon discovered it was played at the White City stadium, an oval arena originally built for the Olympic games in 1923; a bit like an early version of West Ham's ground, complete with a running track and a big capacity of over 50,000. It was situated in Shepherd's Bush, a few miles west of Buckingham Palace and a short walk from the home of Queen's Park Rangers. Unfortunately, it was demolished in the 1980s and for years the site was derelict. Now, Margot was delighted to find out, a huge shopping centre called Westfield had replaced it.

'They've got all the sports shops, a cinema and the best burgers. And we can go tomorrow morning. It's not far away.'

James still had serious doubts. 'But my family has no connection to the World Cup. And where am I going to find a trinket? What even is a trinket?'

'I think it's something small, like an ornament. Maybe Auntie Sue's hiding it from you?' Her eyes widened. 'The shoebox you found under her bed! It could be in there!'

The thought of getting caught again in her room filled James with dread. Losing his house and moving in with the rats on the roundabout was about as appealing as living with the Splatters.

'I'm not going near her room ever again.' he said. 'Not with the smell and those crusty clothes and dead mouse. Besides, I've got to go to Grandad's old house after school and pick up his mail. I promised my dad. Fancy coming?'

Margot agreed. 'But I've got training first. Why don't you come along?'

Chapter 32

His nerves were jangling. He wondered what on earth he was doing there. As did everyone else in the changing room apart from Margot, who had generously lent him some kit to play in (a red and yellow hooped Partick Thistle top, navy Spurs shorts, black Brentford socks). Putting it on had made him feel a bit sick. Getting rid of the ghosts of his allergy was going to take a while. By the time he headed out onto the field he was so nervous his knees were knocking. Mr Smith, wearing an all-red kit, looked surprised to see him.

'James? Is that you?'

'Yes, sir.'

'Aren't you allergic to football?'

James shook his head. Not wanting to cause Auntie Sue any problems, he told Mr Smith he'd made it up as a prank. Mr Smith frowned. 'Bit of a weird prank.'

He gave a false laugh. 'Yes, sir. Shane put me up to it.'

'Like the tag game when you were trying to run out of the school?'

'Exactly.'

'Right, well.' James was thrown a ball, which he held with the tips of his fingers. To the small boy, it felt like a ticking bomb. Mr Smith looked at him, doubtfully. 'At some point you're going to have to stand up to him.'

'Sorry?' said James, blindsided.

'Shane. He gets away with everything because he's big and strong. Just don't believe everything people say.'

'What do you mean?'

'Well, Shane might tell you he's going to do this or that to you, but the chances are, he won't. Some people tell lies. You've got to work out whether to believe them or not.'

James immediately thought of auntie Sue.

'Courage is the key, and Shane won't be back at school 'til Monday.' They joined the team around the centre circle. 'Now, what position do you play?'

'I know, sir' said Blonde Buzzcut. 'Left back. Because he should be left back in the changing room!' Most of the players laughed, but James wasn't really listening because another lost memory had opened up.

I wanted to impress the other players. It was windy. We were wearing tracksuits. I didn't know any of the other kids. I had a ball in my hand. The coach asked us which positions we all liked to play. 'Left midfield, like Martin Peters' I said. 'He's my Grandad's favourite player.'

He blinked his way back to the here and now. 'Left midfield, sir. Like Martin Peters.'

The Buzzcut boys cracked up laughing. 'Martin who?!'

'He scored for England in the World Cup Final.'

'You know your stuff.' said Mr Smith with a wink.

'Shame he ain't got the bucks for a decent kit,' said Blonde Buzzcut.

James popped a yellow bib over his striped top. It was seven-a-side. He moved across to the left wing and stood just inside the touchline. He looked at the faded lines marking out the pitch and they felt familiar to him. He'd definitely stood around this mark before. It didn't stop him feeling a bit sick. His stomach was doing somersaults. Was the allergy returning? Margot called him over and told him to calm down.

'You look like you're gonna puke.'

'I feel like it.'

The first match kicked off and James touched the ball three times. Once by accident – it hit him on the shin – once on purpose after Margot had passed to him and he accidently kicked it into touch and the third time the ball bounced off head into his own goal. He sat out the rest of the matches and waited on the touchline, gawping at how amazing his new friend was. She made everything look so effortless. Her balance, power and pace were head and shoulders above every other player. Her skills were mesmerizing, so enchanting that for a while he forgot all about not being allergic to faartboil.

'Faartboil'. Was it necessary to continue calling it that? There he was, sitting on the grassy bank in full football kit, watching a game of football, having played it himself for fifteen minutes. His breathing was normal, he no longer felt queasy, and his skin was soft to the touch. There was nothing wrong with him. He gazed up to the bruised, cloudy sky and mouthed the word 'football'. He waited for something to happen; for his skin to turn scaly or giant ears sprout from his head, but none of those things happened. In fact, he felt pretty good. He said it again, whispering the word. Then again, speaking quietly, and finally he shouted it loud, again and again, jumping up and down the bank. The players stopped and gawped. Mr Smith stared at him, his whistle falling from his mouth. James blushed.

'Erm.' His throat felt sticky. 'You're playing football. See?' He pointed an unconvincing finger towards the ball on the pitch. The players looked at each other, bemused.

'Very good. Now, keep practising...' Why was his mouth still moving? 'your football...skills. Football. Not faartboil. Very important not to get them confused.'

Omar raised his hand. 'Sir, I think James is the only confused one.'

Chapter 33

The first thing James noticed about grandad's old house was that the iron gate was now red, as was the front door. They used to be black. New chequered tiles had been laid on the path. Also, the garden itself looked different, with tall shrubs and gravel replacing the narrow lawn and rose bushes. All these changes made the house feel like it had never belonged to his grandfather.

'Why are we here?' said Margot, fixing up her ponytail.

'My dad told me to pick up grandad's letters. I dunno why, he's been dead for a few years.' He pushed open the gate and wandered up the path to the front door, giving the doorbell a quick press. They waited.

'I don't think anyone's in' said Margot. Suddenly the door opened, and James spun round to see a withered old man with round glasses standing in the doorway.

'Hello?' he said. 'What do you want?'

A woman's voice shouted loudly from inside. 'Who is it, Gurpreet?'

The man responded by shouting back to her. 'I don't know. There's two of them. Schoolgirls.'

James cleared his throat. 'Actually, I'm a boy.'

'Oh,' said the man, at normal volume, before cranking it up to ten again. 'One of them says they're a boy.'

'What do they want?' she hollered.

Wishing to keep his eardrums intact, James stepped back. 'Do you have any post?'

The man looked him up and down, suspiciously. 'He's trying to sell us a lamp post.'

'Tell him we don't want one.'

'No,' said James. 'I'm not selling a lamp post.'

'He hasn't got any left,' barked the man to his wife.

'Then how can he sell us one?!'

The man glared at James and dropped his voice slightly. 'Then how can you sell us one?'

'Sorry' said James, taking a deep breath. 'My grandad used to own this house before you. His name was Ronald Eligus. And I wondered if you've got some of his post?'

The man's face softened a little. He scratched his head, rolling the name around in his head. 'Ronald Eligus.' He repeated over and over. Then he twisted his neck towards the hall and boomed in a scratchy voice.

'Did Roland Elephant live here before us? The boy wants to know if we got a free post when we brought the house?'

James let out a big sigh. Margot shrugged. The sound of shuffling feet on carpet came from inside and an old woman in a beautiful crimson sari appeared, hunched over a cane. She gazed up at the visitors over half-moon glasses. With a smack of the lips, she shoved her husband out of the way and opened the door fully. 'You say your grandfather used to live here?'

James nodded.

'What was his name?'

'Ronald Eligus.'

She nodded. 'So, you're his grandson?'

'Yes.'

'We don't want a lamp post. There's plenty on this street. Don't try and sell us things we already have.'

James turned to leave.

'But wait,' she called, 'there's some old junk mail you can have. I've been telling my lazy husband to drop it over for months, but he is too bone idle.' The man protested from behind the door. The woman threw her hands up. 'Don't just stand there, lazy bones. Go and fetch the boy's letters!'

He hurried through the hall and returned a few moments later, handing James a bundle of envelopes. Without another word, the woman nodded a swift goodbye and slammed the door shut, making a plant pot fall off the windowsill.

Chapter 34

They stopped on the street corner as James flicked through his grandfather's post; brochures for cruises, offers of credit cards and various membership pamphlets.

'What you got?' asked Margot.

'Just junk mail. Nothing inter...' He suddenly froze.

'What is it?'

Right at the back of the pile, he uncovered a small brown parcel with a handwritten address.

'This one's for me. It's in my dad's handwriting.'

'Your dad sent you a letter addressed to your dead grandad's house?'

He nodded. 'Pretty weird, eh?' He tore it open and read:

> The answers are in the beach ball.
> xxxx

James pushed his hand into the envelope and drew out what looked like a flattened piece of plastic cake. Realizing this was the beach ball, he quickly blew it up. The colours were faded green, red and white, as was the 'Mexico '70' logo and cartoon mascot. It was in excellent condition, as though it had never been played with. Written across one of the white segments was the following score-line:

FINAL:
BRAZIL 4 – ITALY 1
Pele (18)   Boninsegna (37)
Gerson
Jairzinho
Carlos Alberto

Margot pulled out her phone and began tapping at the screen. 'That was the result of the Mexico 1970 World Cup final.'

James had a flashback, watching the match at Grandad's house. Brazil in their famous canary yellow tops and the azure blue of Italy, on the yellowy turf of the Azteca stadium.

'Grandad said this Brazil team were the best international side of all time.' He threw the ball to Margot who juggled it with her head.

'Hey, wait!' She rattled it. 'There's something inside.' They gazed at each other, ominously. Standing by the kerb, James sliced it open with a jagged stone and removed a small chrome key. A white piece of paper had been sellotaped to it with '7 B'Bridge' written in tiny letters.

'This must mean 7 Brightbridge Road?' said James.

'There's no houses along there. Just garages.'

Chapter 35

Before them stood a rickety blue garage door, with the number '7' painted in the top corner. It was the most unremarkable garage door in the history of garage doors. James had literally walked past it every day since he'd started at St Mark's. He pushed the key into the lock of the rusty handle, and, to his delight, it slid in effortlessly.

'Well go on, open it!' urged Margot.

He wriggled the rusty chrome handle, but it refused to twist. He tried again, and again. 'Come onnnn!' He hissed.

'Let me have a go.' offered Margot. 'We had a garage back in Scotland. My dad said there was a knack to it. Lift the handle up and twist it,' she demonstrated, 'then push the top of the door with your spare hand and...'

With an ear-splitting grind of metal, the door swung open and disappeared through slit at the top. However, instead of finding a dark room full of cobwebs and soggy boxes, they were confronted with another door, only this one was made of steel.

'What the...?' they gawped. This door looked like it belonged in a bank vault or a science fiction movie. Heavy, impenetrable steel and little else other than an LED display which invited them to ENTER CODE.

'What do you think the passcode could be?'

'Your date of birth?'

He tapped it in. A displeasing 'BLURP' sounded out.

Margot tapped her chin. 'Do you know any of your parents' dates birth? What about your grandad's?'

He threw his hands up in the air. 'No. I don't know them. Do you know your grandad's date of birth?'

'You can't give up!' she said. 'The answer's got to be somewhere.'

James sighed. 'The chances of us guessing a six figure passcode without a single clue is almost impossible.'

'Almost, not absolutely.'

'The only thing we've got is that stupid beach ball. I mean, we can't even play with it.' He picked the floppy piece of plastic off the floor and gave it a glance. 'Wait a sec.' He pointed to the score line.

```
FINAL:
BRAZIL 4 - ITALY 1
Pele (18)              Boninsegna (37)
Gerson
Jairzinho
Carlos Alberto
```

'That's dad's handwriting. He left out the times of some of the goals. Boninsegna's goal for Italy is written, so is Pele's, but not the rest. The missing numbers could be the passcode.'

Margot began tapping on her phone. James rushed to

the keypad and beckoned her to call the scorers and times, in chronological order.

'First goal was Pele on eighteen minutes, then the equaliser in the thirty-seventh, then Gerson on sixty-six, Jairzihno on seventy-one and finally Roberto Carlos in the eighty-sixth minute.'

James pushed in the numbers **6-6-7-1-8-6**.

They felt a deep rumbling vibration coming from the pavement. Their mouths dropped. The keypad lit up with a satisfying 'PING'. Both slowly glanced down at the shaky floor with huge, mystified eyes. Then suddenly the steel door fell through the floor and disappeared entirely, leaving a very dusty, dark, silent opening. Once they'd stopped coughing, they peered inside, waiting for their eyes to adjust to the inky darkness. A female computer voice suddenly urged them to 'ENTER! YOU HAVE FIVE SECONDS. FIVE – FOUR - THREE...' Sharing a fascinated glance, they quickly stepped over the threshold as a neon sign lit up against the back wall welcoming them to the 'JULES RIMET NERVE CENTRE'.

Chapter 36

As soon as their feet landed, the steel doors flew up behind them and strips of LED lights from floor to ceiling lit up the room. It was a neat and modern space, certainly nothing like the inside of a regular garage. There wasn't a rusty spanner or dusty cobweb in sight. This place was more like a high-tech office. Two more neon signs fizzed to life. On the left, looming over a dotted map of the world was a sign that said, 'SOCCER CENTRES'. On the wall to their right, it said 'THE SEEKERS'. Under this sign was a huge photo collage of shady and sinister looking faces. The most photographed face was undoubtedly Brett Splatter. Straight ahead, under the NERVE CENTRE sign was a wooden desk with two computer screens standing proud. One of them flickered, drawing the kids in with wide eyes.

'Did you see that?' said James.

It flickered once again, then with a great DONG sound the screen lit up fully, showing a typed message.

James,
Welcome to the Nerve Centre, a top-secret home for the Protector of the Jules Rimet trophy.

It was set up by Grandad after the World Cup was saved from the clutches of Brett Splatter in 1983.

He worked undercover to stop the SEEKERS (see wall on right) and help our family friend, Carlita, set up the Soccer schools (see wall on left).

After he died, I took over.

If you are reading this, I have failed.

It is now down to you to recover the trophy.

Everything you need is in this room.

Dad xx

He read it over and over again. Margot kept nudging him saying 'You're the protector' and 'this is all yours!'. But one phrase stood out to him - '**I have failed**'. Dad had failed by heading to Brett Splatter's house. His mind went back to their last night together, to the moment Dad had pointed to the television saying, '*I'm going to rescue that trophy*' and '*It's my duty, and it'll be yours one day.*'

He began thinking aloud. 'Something doesn't make sense. We know that Dad was arrested at the Splatter mansion, which means he believed that Brett Splatter had stolen the trophy. But he was caught with jewellery in his pockets. The police never once mentioned the World Cup.'

'The thing I don't get is why your dad would want to steal jewellery? Were you poor?'

James shook his head. 'I don't think so.'

'And why not just rob a jeweller? Why choose Brett Splatter?'

James shrugged and wandered to the SEEKERS wall

'Why are there so many photos of him? Some of these

go back ages.' He picked off a black and white photo and held it up. 'He's even got hair in this one!'

Margot got up. 'Which means he's been seeking the trophy a long time.'

James nodded. 'He must be desperate by now.' He took a deep breath to gather his thoughts. 'So, right now, we know the trophy is with the drone. But drones don't care about lost trophies, their owners do.'

'So, who is the pilot of the drone?'

James smiled. 'Last night, when it dropped off the second task, it spat out a note saying it was 'a family friend.'

They rushed to the computer, glanced at dad's letter, and cried out. 'CARLITA!'

Both kids were now talking like a roller coaster ride; breathless, fast and seriously excited.

'Remember' said James, 'during the introduction to the Challenge, they talked about soccer schools?'

Margot spun round and pointed to the map. 'Those dots are the schools. Your dad and grandad must have guarded Carlita and the trophy while she set them up. They were like spies!'

James wrinkled his nose.

'But why is Carlita giving it away? Why has she made up this challenge? And why is she giving Brett Splatter a chance to win it?'

'Maybe it's a challenge to you, to see if you're ready, to see if you've got the courage to be her protector?'

James pushed his hair back and blew out a sigh.

'You're right. I've got to win this Challenge.' His eyes suddenly sparkled. 'And I know what to use as my trinket for the next round!'

Standing by the desk, he opened the top drawer and lifted out a small, battered furry toy lion wearing a faded union jack top.

'Margot, meet Wills. His real name is World Cup Willy.'

'Hi' said Margot, unimpressed. 'What's that? It's got no hair and only one eye!'

'He's old.' said James, stroking its head. 'This was England's mascot for the '66 World Cup.'

'Riiight. Looks like it could have been a mascot for the first Olympic games!'

He held Wills tight and looked around the room. Memories were flooding back. He clambered onto the desk and grabbed a red book from the shelf above.

'This used to be my favourite book. It's all about the 1966 World Cup.' He scrambled down and flipped the book open at a random page. 'I love all the old photos. Wembley Stadium, the goals and turf kicking up.'

Together, they peered at the headline: 'PICKLES THE DOG RESCUES WORLD CUP'. But 'Pickles the dog' had been crossed out and replaced in blue ink with the name 'RON ELIGUS'. Stuck to the right-hand page was a loose black and white newspaper cutting. Accompanying the headline 'BOY REWARDED FOR WORLD CUP RESCUE' was a photo of a boy holding World Cup Willy in one hand and a small gold coin in the other.

He was wearing roller skates. The caption read:

'10-year-old Ronald Eligus discovered the trophy under a holly bush in Battersea Park, wrapped in newspaper. 'At first, I thought it was a bag of chips,' said Ronald 'but when I tore off a strip and saw a gold wing, I instantly knew what I'd found.' The young football fan skated across the park and headed for the nearest police station. However, just as he was leaving the entrance gate, the poor boy tripped over a paving slab and knocked himself out. The trophy skidded under a car and was found by a curious dog named Pickles.'

'Your grandad found the World Cup after it had been stolen in 1966?' said Margot, shocked.

'Yes!' said James, as another memory flooded back. 'That's why he loved the trophy so much. But how did he get to know Carlita?'

Just then, they heard a series of loud bangs against the door from outside. James threw his finger to his lips and they both crouched down under the desk. There were voices now; deep, London accents. Unknown to them, it was Les and Brian. This is what they heard:

'There's a passcode.'

'How many letters?'

'Six.'

'What six letter words are there?'

'Football.'

'Football doesn't have six letters! It has…more.'

'Oh, the keypad only has numbers, mate.'

'How many six letter numbers are there?'

''One' has three letters. 'Two' has three letters. They've all got three letters, mate.'

'It wants us to put in six numbers.'

'Oh, I see. Try your mum's birthday.'

They heard a BLURP sound.

'What about Mr Splatter's birthday.'

'You've got to be joking. Ron Eligus hated him.'

'Try it anyway.'

Another BLURP sound.

'What about all the 'ones'.'

BLURP

'All the 'twos'?'

BLURP

'Why don't we just smash it down?'

'Good idea!'

CRASH! BANG! CRASH!

'Solid, that. Shall we go and get some chips? I'll get young Shaney a battered sausage.'

Brett Splatter's heavyweights gave the door one last BANG. Then, with a huff and a tyre screech they sped away down the road. Neither child dare move until the sound of the engine had completely dissolved. Once satisfied, they stuffed their rucksacks with paperwork and got out quickly.

Chapter 37

As the morning sun rose into a cloudless sky, James woke to find a pink letter attached to his cheek. His head was still spinning from the unfurling revelations of yesterday, and as he peeled the page from his face, he felt the need to read it again to make sure he understood it fully.

27 November 1983

Hi Ron,

The Jules Rimet trophy has now sat in the same cabinet in the same corridor for thirteen years. The world's most famous trophy has been forgotten. I snuck into the offices and saw it the other day. There are cobwebs on its wings. Why does no-one polish it? Don't you feel angry about this? I do.

That's why I'm hatching a plan to take it. I know you don't want me to. I know you think it's wrong, but I'd be doing it for a good cause. Remember your dream for the trophy when we were young? To have a competition where a different child would win it every four years? Maybe, we will do this one day, but for now, I am going to take the cup, raise lots of money and build soccer centres in poor towns around the world. Surely, it's better than letting the trophy rot in a cabinet.

Yours,

Carlita

James and Margot walked through the park heading to Ealing Broadway Tube Station. Both were wearing rucksacks stuffed with paperwork from the Nerve Centre and both were eager to share their findings.

'She took the cup because it had been forgotten. She felt so strongly that it should be celebrated' said James. 'But that's not all. I found an even better letter.' They sat down on a park bench as James delved into his bag and handed it to his friend.

29 December 1983
Hi Ron,
Merry Christmas!
I have hidden the trophy in my grandma's house. No-one will find it. It's in a shoebox under her bed. I know you didn't want me to take it, but I had no choice.

You told me that Brett Splatter was in Rio to steal the cup. For three days I watched people go in and out of the football headquarters. Finally, just as it was closing, he appeared, dressed as a cleaner. He was stopped by two security guards and kept outside as his I.D. was checked.

I had no time to lose. I hurried into the building through an open fire escape and raced up the stairs to the third floor. The trophy was on display in a small glass cabinet along the corridor and when I saw it, I nearly cried. It was covered in dust and cobwebs! I slipped on my gloves, opened the cabinet door, and took it out. I couldn't believe the cabinet wasn't locked. It was like taking cheese from the fridge. Lowering the trophy into a shopping bag of cotton wool, I headed for the fire escape. There, I removed my wig and changed my beige work jacket for a navy coat and hurried down the steps. The fire exit led me out into a bustling street of Christmas shoppers. From there, I headed to a large square, where people were singing hymns around a Christmas tree. A few minutes later I heard a faint alarm sound and guessed Brett Splatter must have set it off.

The next morning, as you know, the world woke up to the news that the trophy had once again been stolen. I woke up wondering If I'd done the right thing. I've never stolen anything before, not even a sweet. I've just taken one of the world's most valuable things and I know that many dangerous people will pursue me, especially Brett Splatter.

Ron, you are the only one who knows and the only one who can help me.

Please don't tell anyone else.

C x

Chapter 38

The tube journey to Westfield went by in a flash. Sat in a near empty carriage at the front, they put all their notes and diaries from the Nerve Centre on the spare seat between them and continued discussing their findings. As the train rattled along, the two friends pieced together what they'd learnt so far.

'Grandad found out that Brett Splatter was planning to steal the trophy and told Carlita.'

'She waited outside the building. And then…'

'…Splatter turned up, dressed as a cleaner.'

'She beat him to it.'

'And Grandad set up the Nerve Centre to protect Carlita and watch Brett Splatter and other baddies.'

They high fived each other and continued picking at the paperwork.

'Oh.' cried Margot, making him almost jump out of his seat. 'You need to see this!' She passed him a document that looked like a certificate. The writing style reminded him of Shakespeare. Even though he could tell it was only a few years old, there was a regal quality to its appearance.

'This is to certify that George Eligus succeeds Ronald Eligus as the official Protector of the Jules Rimet Trophy. As the new Protector, George Eligus has vowed to keep secret all knowledge of the whereabouts of the Jules Rimet Trophy. He will never speak of the trophy nor jeopardise it in any way.'

The tube ground to a halt at Shepherd's Bush station. As shoppers, dressed in shorts and summer dresses, bustled in and out of the carriage, the kids stuffed their rucksacks with the paperwork and stepped onto the escalator. James took in none of his surroundings; his mind was otherwise engaged.

'That's why Dad didn't tell the police he was looking for the trophy when he was caught! He made a vow of silence! Splatter must have known about his secret.'

'Do you think the old baldie might have planted the jewellery in his pockets and maybe punched him or something?'

James stared at her. 'Do you think someone could really be that horrible?'

Chapter 39

Westfield Shopping Centre is enormous. It is officially the largest shopping centre in the whole of Europe and would fit roughly thirty football pitches inside. As James stepped onto its marble-floored, glass-roofed glory, he was amazed by the sheer hugeness of what lay before him. He gazed at the giant steel trees that held up the giant glass wavy roof. He watched a lady, reclined in a thick white chair in the centre of a big walkway, having her nails painted. Small children were being pushed around by tall adults in cool little cars. A dance music track blared loudly from the main concourse below them. Margot grabbed his arm, and they found a space by the glass barrier overlooking the stage. There a pretty, young pop starlet was midway through one of her favourite cover songs.

'It's like a music festival,' said James, as Margot pulled him away to show him around the sports shops.

As morning dwindled and the crowds of shoppers increased, they decided it was time to find **SEAT No: 278 West Stand Upper Tier.**

It didn't take them long to work out that they were already on the first floor, what they imagined to be the Upper Tier. Then it was just a case of finding shop number 278 in the West Stand. As there were no stands, they plumped to just find shop 278 instead. Shop 276 belonged to Pret A Manger. They were close. Next to Pret on the left was Banana Republic, which, to James's disappointment, sold clothes not bananas. Next to it on the right was another clothes store called Zara.

They stood outside the entrance to Pret looking this way and that, getting jostled by weekend shoppers eager to avoid the heatwave. For a few scary moments James lost Margot as he was bundled towards the Zara entrance in a mini stampede. He felt increasingly small and hopeless and young. Once re-united, they took it in turns to check the marble floor tiles for clues. They peered at the entrances of Pret and Banana Republic and Zara, all the time being swept around like autumn leaves in a park.

'It's no use' said James, wearily. 'It's too busy. And I've got to be back by one o'clock.'

'Five more minutes. It has to be here somewhere' said Margot, leaning against a billboard displaying a map of the shopping centre. They looked around aimlessly for a while, thinking, hoping a clue might jump out at them. Then James noticed the map, which was literally right next to him. It was split into three sections; there was a floor plan showing where each shop was situated. There were two floors to this enormous place, so two maps. And then there were little arrows by each exit saying 'CAR PARK'. And at the bottom, it advertised proudly that there were over a thousand numbered car park spaces on five levels.

'We haven't checked the car park' he said, with renewed

energy. 'This map says the car park spaces are numbered. It's worth a try, and it won't be so busy.'

They snaked through the throng of summer shoppers, down escalators and through doors until they reached an information desk in the car park concourse.

'Can I help?' said a man in a suit.

'We're looking for space number 278.' said Margot, leaning confidently over the counter. 'Our mum told us to meet her there.'

The man tapped on his computer. 'Yes, it's on this floor.' He pointed through the clear doors into the car park. 'If you go out at this entrance and go straight on for about fifty metres, you'll see a sign saying 'C2'. Turn left, and it's eight spaces along.'

They flung open the doors and sprinted towards their destination, passing the signs C17, 16,15 and so on, until, reaching C2. Aside from the occasional echo of car engines, all was quiet. But there was something about this eerie quiet that heightened his emotions and suddenly James began to feel tense. Space number 278 was empty and entirely unremarkable. It was, after all, just a rectangular parking space with straight white markings and a painted number on the black floor like all the others.

However, on closer inspection, in the centre of the upper circle of the number '8', was an unmarked brushed chrome disc, about the size of a cricket ball. With hearts pounding they bent down on their knees and ran their fingers over it. No inscriptions, no markings whatsoever. Just a round disc in the floor. Frustratingly, James stood up and kicked it.

'Let's go' he said, turning away.

'Wait,' said Margot, her words echoing around the car park. 'Something's happening!'

The disc revolved slowly, with a quiet squeak. There followed a mechanical click, then a whirr, and then the disc rose from the floor to reveal a solid brushed steel cylinder about a foot high. It looked like a silver Pringles tin. There was another click and from within the cylinder, a small door opened with the words **PLACE TRINKET HERE** on the front. James took out Wills, squeezed it into the cylinder and shut the door. With a click and a whirr, the cylinder slowly disappeared into the floor. They looked at each other. James was worried.

'Do you think Wills will be ok?'

'Aye. 'Course he will. It's Carlita's competition. She was your grandad's friend. She's not gonna do anything bad to it, is she.' James nodded, uncertainly. The silence was broken by the rising sound of a car engine.

'That space free?' said the lady driver.

'Er, no.' said James, thinking of an excuse. 'We're holding it for our parents. We always park in the same space. It's a tradition.' He offered his best and most charming smile. The lady, after what seemed like an eternity, reluctantly accepted his excuse with a tut, and drove off. James felt his tummy rumble.

'What's happened to Wills? What if the machine breaks? We'll never get him back.'

'Stop worrying.'

They stared intently at the silver disk on the floor, hoping it would do something soon. Then another car pulled up. 'Is that space free?' asked a man, popping his head over the car bonnet.

'No!' said James, annoyed at the interruption.

'Sorry, we're waiting for our parents' said Margot, giving him a nudge. The man sighed heavily and sped off. Just then, with a relieving click, the cylinder on the floor in front of them turned slowly, and with a gentle whirring noise, rose to its full height. With a snap, the door swung open, and Wills spilled out. Then something else ejected onto the ground, landing with a tinkle. A gold-coloured pendant in the shape of the Jules Rimet trophy. James joyfully picked up his prize with – **YOU WIN! 10 POINTS** – engraved on the back. Just then, another car pulled up. Margot rolled her eyes and without looking, shouted at the driver.

'We're waiting for our parents!'

'It must be your parents, Margot' said Brett Splatter, leaning from the window of his black Rolls-Royce, 'because I know one of his is in jail.'

Chapter 40

A sudden feeling of déjà-vu struck James as Shane emerged from the back seat with a manic look on his face. He was going to have to run for his life again. But there was another thing nagging him, something that baffled and almost outraged him.

'How did you know to come here? How did you work it out?'

'It wasn't hard' said Brett Splatter, slamming his door shut with a loud echo.

'Nah,' agreed Shane. 'Grandad got some football professor bloke to solve it.'

'You cheated!'

'No, he never' said Les and Brian, muscles bulging from their t-shirts.

Shane shrugged. 'Can you see a ref giving me a red card?' He looked around. 'Nope. So come on, hand over the prize. I want my ten points.'

'You've got to be joking' said Margot. 'Run, James. Split up!'

There was a moment's hesitation as his legs waited for the message to get through.

'Right' said James, scurrying off in the opposite direction between two parked cars.

'Where are you, Fleubler?' growled Shane, prowling around the static vehicles. His voice echoing off the low, concrete ceiling.

With Wills back in his bag, James carefully hooked the rucksack over his shoulder and peered through various car windows watching out for his nemesis. He could feel his heart pulsing and sweat trickling down his back. The entrance was a good distance away. With the bag weighing him down, Shane would easily catch him in a straight race. But he had one advantage that might just help him to safety. He was small. Smaller than the car bonnets, which meant he was difficult to find.

With renewed confidence, James scurried from car to car, edging ever closer to the lights of the glass concourse. It was hot and sticky. Car fumes and the smell of tarmac filled his nostrils. The rucksack bashed against his back like a lead pendulum. The entrance was tantalisingly close now. Had he out-manoeuvred Shane? He hadn't heard any heavy footsteps or loud sneaker squeaks. Now he was just one car away. He glanced through the windows and saw the man at the information desk. There was an automatic sliding door straight ahead, only a few metres away. Then, from the corner of his eye, Margot appeared, squeezed the doors and sprinted up the escalator away from the flailing Les and Brian, who shook their heads and clutched their knees. For a few moments they skulked around the concourse like confused tigers who had lost their dinner. Finally, they wandered outside, and split up in search of their boss.

It was time to make a move.

James emerged from behind a hatchback and sprinted at full speed towards the doors. Just as they opened Shane charged in from the left. In a flash and a thump, James felt the full force of his arch enemy as Shane rugby tackled him to the floor.

'Gotcha!' he cheered, pinning James down. Reams of papers fluttered free from the rucksack. Brian and Les appeared, panting heavily.

'Why haven't you got Margot?' said Shane, pinning the small boy to the floor.

'She's too fast!' puffed Brian.

Shane dragged James to his feet. Seeing a concerned look from the man on the information desk, he ruffled James' hair and dragged him behind a large truck. The giant boy peered inside the rucksack. 'What's all this? Homework? You're such a nerd! Who brings schoolwork to Westfield?'

Last to arrive was the fake tanned game show host. James was surrounded. A bitterness tasted in his mouth.

'Why have you brought this tatty old thing?' said Shane, holding up Wills.

'No!' cried James, jumping for it and missing.

'And there's this medal thing. Any good to you?' said Brian, taking out the winning Jules Rimet pendant.

'Yesss' said Shane, grabbing it. 'I've won the task now, fake allergy boy!'

'Give it back!'

Brian and Les collected the loose papers from the floor and handed them to Brett Splatter.

'This all looks interesting.' he said and held up a photograph of himself. 'This is me when I was young! I was sooo handsome don't you think fellas?' His face and tone changed as he glared at James and raised a threatening finger. 'Where did you get this, boy?'

James glared back, refusing to speak. His legs felt wobbly.

'Giving me the silent treatment, eh? No matter. Now, let's see what some of this paperwork is.' Brett Splatter cast his eyes down and after a few more dreadful seconds, threw his head back in splendid realization. 'Wait…' he said with a big, fat grin. 'This is all information on the lost trophy; the people searching for it, the places they set up soccer schools. That's why there's a photo of me. It's all here.' He pointed to the quivering boy. 'Have you been playing in your grandad's Nerve Centre?'

Although he didn't say anything, Brett Splatter must have seen a flash of acknowledgement on the boy's face because the old man began chuckling.

'You have. Interesting. So, why don't you be a good little boy and tell Uncle Brett the passcode?' James gritted his teeth and shook his head. The old man grabbed him. 'Not good enough. Tell me, NOW!' His voice echoed through the car park. It gave James an idea.

'HELP! HELP!' he cried. In a moment, the concierge looked up from his desk and picked up the phone. In addition, Margot appeared at the top of the escalator, saw where the noise was coming from and hurried down the steps. Brett Splatter was spooked.

'Get everything in the bag, quick,' he panted.

'Let's take him with us!' said Shane.

'There's people coming.' hissed his grandfather, edging away. 'Get in the car and let's go!'

'Cheers Fleurbler' said Shane, fleeing to the Rolls. The sound of car doors slamming was followed by an engine revving up followed by tyres screeching. James fell to his knees as Margot arrived to comfort him.

Chapter 41

'Hello James. Hello. Hello. James?' The boy stirred. 'James. Wake up.'

Softly. Spoken. South American female voice. White light. Brett Splatter. Wills gone.

'James.'

He opened his eyes, slowly.

'Aaagh!' He sat bolt upright, panting heavily. The silver drone was hovering a few feet away from him. He felt the gentle breeze of its copter blades.

'What the…?' he croaked, pulling the covers up.

'I'm sorry to wake you.'

He blinked, opened his eyes wide, blinked again and wiped his mouth free of dribble. The drone was so close he could see the tiny round criss-cross speaker on the underside of its nose. He checked the time on his stereo - 2.45am.

'Your next task, task three, is on your bed.'

'Get out!' He hissed, suddenly angered. The drone retreated to the window. 'This is all your fault, CARLITA!' he said, hissing her name. 'I've lost all my family secrets now because of you. Now get lost and leave me alone!'

The drone hovered quite still, just out of the boy's reach

'You won task two fair and square. The ten points are

yours. But because valuable information has been leaked, I must take precautions. Go to the Nerve Centre immediately and turn on computer number two. The password is...' The drone spat out a tiny card containing a series of numbers and letters. 'On the desktop you'll find a document marked 'James', this is for you to read. Shut down everything after. Splatter will be on your tail. Oh, and the last time I saw you, football was your life. Remember this.'

The short walk to the Nerve Centre in his faded Iron Man onesie was a tense one. He was surprised to find that, even though it was the dead of night, it wasn't that dark. The moon was full and sky clear. All the way there he kept his keen eyes out for suspicious behaviour, but the streets were empty, and as he tapped in the code to the Nerve Centre with shaky fingers, the only living thing he saw was a fox, scurrying behind a parked car. As instructed, he switched on the computer, found the file, opened the document, and began to read:

Dear James,
Your father was a very committed Protector. He had trained under grandad Ron for five years and was very skilled in surveillance security. However, the poor man also had a job and a son to look after. Some nights he would come to the nerve centre with you asleep in the pushchair and carefully watch over me on a grainy computer screen until dawn. Then, he'd take you home, feed you breakfast, put you in the car seat and drive to work. You were his constant companion and his closest friend.

One morning, a little over two years ago, disaster struck. I was carrying the trophy on a trip to Switzerland. Because I need to stay hidden, I have many different names and passports. Your father knew them all, but this time I decided to use a new name and didn't tell him what it was.

We had a routine: When I landed after every flight, I always called his mobile and hung up after two rings if things were ok. If I suspected problems, I would not ring at all. That day I didn't call, because as soon as we landed, I slumped forward in my seat and fell unconscious. I was having a heart attack.

Your father's phone was switched off as he was at one of your school assemblies. He knew exactly where I was going. As soon as it finished and he discovered there were no missed calls from me, he rushed instantly to the Nerve Centre. He called, emailed, and texted. He made sure the flight had arrived on time. He even tapped into the CCTV cameras at the airport, but he was too late. An ambulance had taken me to a hospital outside the city. He checked all passenger information with the airline. He checked hospitals, police stations, using all my alias names. But crucially, he didn't know the right one because I'd forgotten to give it to him.

For the next three weeks I was unconscious. Those three weeks would prove devastating to both you and your father. Brett Splatter had been secretly following your dad and discovered that contact had been lost between us.

Sensing his opportunity, he sent an anonymous email stating that the Jules Rimet trophy had been discovered at his mansion. As your dad couldn't get in touch with me, he believed the information, and, well, you know the rest.

The boulder in his throat was painful. Hot, stingy tears fell down his cheeks. Brett Splatter had framed Dad after all. He wiped his nose on his sleeve and carried on reading:

I woke up, three weeks later in a strange hospital, in a strange bed. Thankfully, the trophy was still safely hidden in my suitcase. But I was scared. Then I discovered that my Protector had been caught stealing jewellery from Brett Splatter's house and faced eight years in prison.

You were now without a father, and I was without protection. For the first time since I took the trophy, I was vulnerable and regretful that I was vowed to silence.

Then, Brett Splatter sent me an email and my heart almost stopped forever. He was getting closer to the trophy. I needed to slow him down. Knowing he had a grandson and that you loved football, I presented your grandad's idea, of a Jules Rimet challenge offering children the chance to win the trophy. He jumped at it, obviously convinced that Shane would win.

Because I was working alone it took a long time organize. I am sorry that I haven't been able to help you. I cannot turn back time, but if you win, I will hand myself in to the police, rip up the stupid vow of silence, and tell them everything. Hopefully it will help release your father from prison.

I hope to see you again very soon.

Carlita xx

Chapter 42

Dear James,
The score after round two is:
SHANE 4 – JAMES 16
TASK 3:
CROSSBAR CHALLENGE. You will recreate Geoff Hurst's second goal from the 1966 Final. Players will take it in turns to cross the ball while the other attempts to shoot, hitting the underside of the crossbar before scoring. 10 points for scoring off the bar, 5 points to hit crossbar, 2 points for a goal, 1 point for a good cross.
2PM TODAY at the SANDY PARK.

It was a muggy, overcast day. Thick, heavy clouds bulged at the seams with rain. James hadn't noticed. He'd spent most of the morning in his room listening to Dad's favourite old records and practising for the latest task using rolled up socks as a ball. The crossbar was the shelf above his bed. He soon found out, however, that it was pretty difficult to swivel and shoot like Geoff Hurst. That was the first thing. Secondly, there was no-one to cross the sock. Thirdly, he kept bashing his foot against the

154

bedframe, stereo or bedside table. Fourthly, the sock-ball kept unravelling. Imagining Brett Splatter as the sock ball, he threw it up and swung a foot at it. Finally, it smacked against the shelf, bounced back and landed on his stereo. The digital clock blinked at him. 'Blimey,' he thought. It was 1.21pm and he needed to get ready. Diving under his bed he threw on some joggers and jumper to hide his kit.

He opened the living room door to find Auntie Sue gazing into a mirror, putting make-up on. In all the time she'd lived in his house, he'd never seen her wearing make-up She was clearly out of practise. It looked as though she'd just been splatted with a multi-coloured paint gun.

'Are you going out?' he asked.

'Might be.'

'With anyone I know?'

She chuckled to herself. 'You might.'

'It's just that...' he paused, knowing what he was about to say might mean losing dad's phone call this week, '...I've been invited to Margot's for Sunday lunch.'

'Fine with me' she replied, smearing lipstick across her mouth area. James was stunned. Then the doorbell rang.

'I'll get it!' they cried at the same time. James rushed to the door first, such was his curiosity on what her new 'friend' looked like.

'Hello Possum...Oh, James' said Brett Splatter.

'You!' cried James in disbelief. He spun round to see Auntie Sue, who was blushing slightly. 'Is that your 'friend'?!'

'He is' she said tipping her head to one side.

'He's evil. He's ruined this family!'

Auntie Sue let out a nervous chuckle. 'You wouldn't do that, would you Brett?'

'Of course not, my dear.'

'And besides, he treats me nice.' said Auntie Sue, swooning.

James couldn't believe his ears. In a fit of rage, he shoved past Brett Splatter and escaped down the path. He sprinted as fast as he could to the Sandy Park, arms pumping fists crunching legs thumping. He'd never felt so angry. How could she make such a bad decision? How long had this been going on?

A light drizzle rained down. The park was deserted which felt good. He felt better being alone and he liked the feeling of the gentle rain on his face. It helped him calm down. He started thinking about something Carlita had said in her letter. She came up with the idea for this competition to stop Brett Splatter's advances on the trophy. He accepted because obviously, he thought he was going to win. That must have been around two years ago. This was the same time James was told he was allergic to football. This led him to another thought; had Brett Splatter created the football allergy to stop James taking part in the challenge?

Chapter 43

Shane booted another new football high into the air, giving James a threatening look. He was getting bored with Shane and his stupid looks.

'Pass the ball?' Shane ignored him. 'Shane?' He watched the huge boy in his snug Real Madrid kit attempt a few keepy-uppies.

Then, remarkably, Auntie Sue waddled past with her head bowed under a 'Measure the Treasure' hoodie. 'WHAT IS SHE DOING HERE?????'

He froze. He thought about running away. He thought about climbing the nearest tree and disappearing among the leaves; or building a brick wall, digging a big hole, making wings. He took another glance, but, incredibly, she paid him no attention whatsoever. Surely, she knew he was there. Apart from Shane, he was the only kid on the field.

She slumped down on the bench under the big oak tree, facing away from the action. Brett Splatter took a seat next to her, but she pushed him away. Throwing an arm up, the old man, wearing a long navy coat, got up and stood behind the goal.

'Do some stretches, Shaney.' He clapped, trying to look like a football coach.

'Get lost.'

'Are you James Eligus?' said a short, athletic man wearing a black referee's kit. His face was familiar. His dreadlocks were long and black and silky and when he ran, they bounced off his shoulders like snakes.

'Yes.'

'Good, my name's Mori and I'm the referee for today's task. Are you ready?'

'Are you from Brazil?' said James, recognizing the accent.

'Yes, and today is not Brazilian weather. Who is your opponent?'

James pointed to Shane, who was leaning over his ball, shouting at it.

'Ok, good. Let's get started.'

James followed his gaze into the bruised sky and spotted the drone, looking down from above. They gave each other a knowing look.

The rules were simple. One player would attempt to cross the ball into the box for the other to shoot onto the crossbar. One touch was allowed to control the ball before shooting. Each player was given five chances to cross and five chances to score. One point would be awarded for a good cross, two points for a goal, five points to hit the crossbar. If any player managed to hit the crossbar, and the ball ricocheted down onto the goal line, they would take all ten points and win the task.

'You've both seen Geoff Hurst's goal from the 1966

final?' said Mori, clutching the ball under his arm. The boys nodded. 'Alan Ball crossed it from the right wing into the heart of the penalty area. Hurst brings the ball down, swivels and...' Demonstrating with graceful ease, Mori smashed a shot onto the underside of the bar. 'Muito bom! Think you can do that?'

James looked on astonished. 'Erm...'

'Easy' said Shane.

Chapter 44

Trying to pump some life into his legs, James jumped up and down by the penalty spot. Shane, the boy mountain, took a few steps forward and hit a low cross towards him. The ball hit James on the side of the shin and bounced into touch. The competition had begun.

'That was a good cross, ref!' Shane shouted.

'Great cross Shaney. One point, surely?' clapped his grandfather.

Mori shook his head. 'The cross needs more height, no points.'

As Brett Splatter threw the ball back to his grandson, Mori went over to James.

'Are you ok? You look nervous.' He was right. James had almost forgotten how to stand up. 'You've done this before.' whispered Mori, reassuringly.

'How do you know?'

'My employer told me.' Mori pointed up to the drone with a subtle finger.

'Carlita?'

Mori put his fingers to his lips and winked.

'Shhh, let it come back to you. It won't take long, it's like riding a bike. Now, try to remember what your father taught you. And breathe. Very important to breath or you die.' He patted James on the shoulder and turned his attention to Shane. 'Ok Shane, let's try again.'

James took a deep breath and shut his eyes tightly. 'Come on, dad.' he said to himself. 'Where are you? I need your help'. His memory door remained shut. Hopelessly, James gazed at the gaping wide, empty goal before him, and beyond that, to the suited figure of Brett Splatter. 'I've got to try'. He told himself. 'If only to show them'. He rolled down his socks, pushed back his long, curly hair and nodded towards Shane. Suddenly, a memory flickered.

'Always try to attack the ball. Take a step forward and either try for the volley or bring it down with your instep and then get a shot away. Don't worry if you miss a few to begin with. Ready?'

The ball flew over. It was a good cross. Watching it like a hawk, James let his body take over. He took a step forward and cushioned the ball at waist height with his left instep. The ball dropped invitingly, and James opened up his body and passed it lightly into the far corner of the goal with his right foot.

He'd scored! In front of Brett Splatter!

The urge to run up to the old man and shout 'YEEEEESSSS!' at his gloomy face was almost unbearable. Instead, he decided to act respectfully and went to collect the ball without celebrating at all.

'Surely a point to Shane, ref? That was a great cross,' cried Brett Splatter, throwing his arms up.

This time, the ref nodded in agreement.

'One point to Shane and two to James. That makes the scores James 18, Shane 5.' He collected the ball from James with a wink, and passed the ball back to Shane, who was crouching moodily on his haunches. 'Ok Shane, when you're ready' said Mori. 'Let's have cross number three.'

'Wait!' cried Brett Splatter, raising a hand. He jogged across the tufted grass and whispered something in Shane's ear. The boy nodded with a grin.

'Ready James?' said Shane.

He was. But the cross sent in was way too high.

'You could have got that,' chuckled Shane.

The next cross bobbled straight along the ground and the final ball sailed straight out of play. 'Must have lost my touch. Sorry about that,' he grinned. Shane had deliberately messed up to stop James scoring more points.

Mori didn't look impressed. He peered up to the drone, raised his eyebrows then shook his head as though he'd just been given bad news. 'OK, swap over.'

Now it was down to James to deliver the crosses. As he was left footed and crossing from the right, he would have to swing them in, curling towards the goal. As he placed the ball down on the patchy earth it started drizzling. Once again, he cast his mind back.

'*Place your standing foot just behind the ball, lean back and strike through it.*'

The first cross had no height to it. It was weak and low and rubbish. His second effort was slightly better but still bounced twice before reaching Shane. His third cross was perfect. Bouncing by the penalty spot, Shane moved forward, let it hit his chest and launched a half-volley high into the goal, only narrowly missing the crossbar.

'What a goal!' cried Brett Splatter punching the air.

'It hit the bar as well ref!' appealed Shane, arms outstretched.

Mori shook his head. 'One point to James, two to Shane. That makes it 19 -7.'

The fourth cross sent over was even better. Perfect weight, perfect height, just perfect. Shane's eyes lit up as he, like Geoff Hurst, raised his right knee, cushioned the ball skilfully and sent a thunderous half-volley against the underside of the crossbar. The ground shuddered. The goalpost, dented from the ferocity of the shot, quivered, creaked and finally fell backwards onto the grass with an almighty CLANG!

Brett Splatter raced across to his grandson with his arms outstretched. Mori, the ref, held both hands up to signify the end of the game and announced:

'Shane is the winner of this round, scoring a maximum TEN POINTS. That changes things significantly. The scores are now James 19, Shane 17.'

'Don't I get anything for the cross?' asked James.

Mori looked up to the drone, put a finger to his ears, then shook his head. 'Shane won the task outright I'm afraid.'

Shane ran up and pressed an L-shaped hand to his forehead. 'LOOOOZER! LOOOOZER!'

Mori shook his head and turned away, pushing a finger to his ear once more. Gathering the boys together he announced, 'I've just been told that an extra TWO POINTS will be awarded to the player who puts the goalpost back up.'

Wasting no time, Shane sprinted across and hoisted the crossbar over his head.

'Come on grandad, get on my shoulders.' Trotting over, the old man clambered onto his grandson's shoulders and began pushing the goal back into position.

James, tired, wet and alone, threw his arms out in despair. 'This is rubbish! You're getting extra points for that?!'

'Go home and cry to your little furry lion.'

'I can't, you nicked it!'

'Oh yeah.' grinned Shane.

Chapter 45

Tired and disheartened, James trudged across the pitch to face his auntie, convinced he'd be grounded for the rest of his life. 'Sorry for playing foot, faart, fleurbler.'

'Is it over?' she grunted. The drawstring of her wet hoody was done up so tight around her face all James could see was a small oval of features.

'Aren't you going to tell me off? Or stop Dad's phone call? Or make me live on a roundabout?'

She stood up wearily, shook her head and blew her nose into a hanky. 'Stupid fleurbler's given me a cold. Let's get out of here.'

They left the park in stony silence. James didn't want to talk to her because her boyfriend was the enemy, the worst possible choice of boyfriend, ever. What if they ended up getting married? Shane would become his step-brother-cousin? And the old man would be his step-father-uncle. A shiver ran down his spine as he considered life as a modern-day Cinderella. He sighed, heavily. And what lay ahead when they got home? Auntie Sue had just watched him playing football, the worst crime he could possibly commit. So why hadn't she lashed out at him? Was she making him wait? Was the waiting game part of her torturous plan? He kept glancing up at her squidgedup face inside that ridiculous 'Measure the Treasure' hoody, but it wasn't giving anything away, apart from the odd outbreak of germs when she sneezed. He rubbed his head, anxiously. Maybe she was waiting for him to apologise? He curled up his nose. No, she could apologise to him for loving Brett Splatter, he decided. They turned left into Brightbridge and crossed the narrow road. The Nerve Centre was just ahead. He made a note not to look suspicious when they passed it. Suddenly, she stopped him with a firm hand.

'Erm,' coughed auntie Sue. His heart thudded. 'listen.' She dug her hands into the pouch of her hoody. 'I, er, see you got over your allergy?'

James nodded. This wasn't what he was expecting. Was it a trap?

'Yes.' he said, as calm as he could muster.

'Right.' she said. 'You must have grown out of it, eh?'

'Guess so.' he replied, frowning. Was that it? Two years of her lying to him, done, just like that?! He was livid.

She shuffled awkwardly, sniffling.

'It hasn't been easy for me, all this er, looking after you and that.'

Not easy for you? I've had to avoid fleurblers from all directions all the time thanks to you!

'You see, when I was young, me and your dad weren't friends. When I was tiny, your grandad used to take me everywhere with him, usually fleurbler matches because he was obsessed with it. Apart from us it was the most important thing in his life.' She sneezed, loudly. 'Then, when I was about ten years old it suddenly stopped, and your brother started getting all the special fleurbler treatment. Grandad still took me to judo and dance classes, but I lost that bond with him. And your dad seemed to love watching me miss out, and he loved the fact that I always had to wash his plate up after dinner because they'd rush off to some stupid match. I felt left out, so I decided to hate fleurbler.' She blew her nose again. 'When I started looking after you, I felt like I was cleaning up after him again and I really didn't want to. It wasn't your fault but...' She broke off and shook her head as she started crying. James felt helpless. Should he give her a hug? 'And then Mr Splatter started coming round to comfort me.'

His eyes filled with fury. 'WHATTT?!'

She turned away, blowing her nose. 'He was good at advice.'

'When? Just after you moved in?' She nodded.

Everything had changed two years ago. And who came onto the scene at exactly that time? Brett Splatter!

'He just came round one day. Said he knew I was a fan.'

'Did he make up my allergy?' Heavy rain bounced off the pavement. She tightened her lips, shivering. Thunder rumbled in the distance. He repeated the question. 'Did he make up my allergy?!'

'Look, I can't.' She started crying again. Big, heaving sobs this time which made him feel bad. He had no idea why he should feel any sympathy whatsoever for this woman, but he couldn't help it. Watching her shivering, sneezing and sobbing, he ran along to the Nerve Centre and punched in the passcode. Once safely inside, he sat her down and handed her a blanket.

'So?' said James. She shook her head. 'What? He didn't tell you to make it up?' He remembered what Mr Smith had said about liars. That you must make your mind up whether to believe people. There was a word for fools like him who believed everything; gullible. Well, not anymore, he decided.

'Not now, James, please.' said his auntie.

'When?'

'Soon, I promise.' They sat in silence for a while.

'What is this place?' she said eventually, gazing around. 'Why are there loads of pictures of Brett up there? Some of these were taken when he lived in Australia.'

He wanted to tell her the truth, to stick the boot in, make her feel guilty for lying to him for so long. '*Your boyfriend is just using you to destroy our family so he can get his hands on the lost trophy. He doesn't love you, he doesn't even like you!*' But when he tried, the words just wouldn't come out.

'This was where grandad used to come and…relax. He must have liked Mr Splatter's TV shows.' he lied. He went on to explain the Nerve Centre as a place that grandad kept his hobby, which was World Cups of the past. He denied knowing anything about the SOCCER SCHOOLS or SEEKERS walls.

'This must have been where him and your dad spent all their spare time.' she sniffed.

He looked around for a tissue and suddenly felt bad for lying to her.

'If you don't want me to play football after the challenge,' he conceded, 'I won't.' She sneezed. 'Are you getting a cold?'

'Only when I'm around stupid fleurbler.' she said.

'Like you're allergic to it.' he joked. He opened a draw and saw a blue cardboard box with the name 'SUE' written on the front. He placed it on the desk, opened the lid and they peered inside. It was full of keepsakes from her childhood; paintings and drawings, swimming and judo certificates, exam results, a lock of orange curly hair, a crumpled envelope with 'milk teeth' written on the front. She picked out her birth certificate, a school photo, aged eight, grinning cheekily.

'I'd just got over chicken pox when that was taken.'

A pin badge saying, 'DADDY'S GIRL', medals galore, judo photos and curiously, a letter from the doctors.

'What's this?' He held it up and read casually.

Chelthorne Valley Surgery –

Dear Sue Eligus,
I regret to inform you that, following your recent test, you have contracted an allergy to football.
Under no circumstances must you participate in this

sport, as the consequences could be fatal. In case of an emergency, dial 999.
Yours Sincerely,
Dr C Reed

Their mouths dropped.

'That must be why Grandad didn't include you in any foot... sorry.' he corrected himself. 'fleurbler stuff. It was because he was protecting you.'

She clutched the letter close to her chest and looked at him with bloodshot eyes. 'I think I need to get this checked out.' she sniffed.

Chapter 46

News came later that night, as James slept, of the final task in the competition. The following morning, during another hot and sticky wander to school, he shoved the postcard into Margot's hands and blew out his cheeks.

Dear James,
The score after round three is:
JAMES 19 - SHANE 19
Your FINAL TASK is as follows: Play for your school team in the Cup Final this Thursday.
Two points will be awarded for an appearance, two points for an assist, four points for a goal.
Good Luck

'Carlita said it was gonna be tough, but this is ridiculous.' he said.

'Come on James.' she nudged him. 'You can do it. You're just a bit rusty, that's all. All you need is three days intense training. And a good left foot. And a good right foot come to that.'

'Hey!'

She giggled. 'But you're gonna have to make up an

excuse to Auntie Sue. The final training session is on Wednesday after school. That's when Mr Smith will decide his squad.'

'She's letting me play, just as long as I don't do it in the house.'

'What?'

'She's the one who's allergic to football!'

As they wandered through the school gates for the beginning of their final week at St Mark's Primary, James brought his friend up to speed with the challenge, his family situation and Carlita's promise.

After cramming down a marmite sandwich at lunchtime, he headed onto the softly melting playing field with his new friends. Two teams of Years Five and Six were battling it out on the main pitch led by Shane. As soon as the cube-headed boy caught sight of James he started laughing.

'You'll never get in the school team, Fleurbler. It's not even worth trying. That trophy's mine!'

The Buzzcut brothers stood either side of him and chanted 'FLEURBLER IS A LOSER!'.

Margot led him away to back of the field, where she took him through reps of squats, shuttle sprints, dribbling exercises and passing drills. Finally, when he could no longer feel his legs, she concluded the session with a penalty shoot-out. As James lined up his first kick, Dad's voice returned.

Pick your spot and stick to it.

Breathe evenly

Don't worry about the keeper. This is between you, the ball and the goal.

He scored one out of five. After school, they went to the Sandy Park for an ice-cream. It was simply too hot to continue training in this heat. While sitting under the mottled shade of a tree, she showed him lots of tips, tricks and skills on YouTube. His enjoyment was cut short when Shane tugged the back of his polo top and made him drop his ice-cream in the sand.

'You carry on playing football, and I'll break your legs. Got that?'

'Come on, Shane.' James was convinced his rival was lying. 'We don't need to be like this.'

But Shane wasn't interested in peace. He just wanted to see James in pieces. The huge oaf tugged at the back of the tiny boy's long locks to ram home his point.

'I mean it. If I see you playing tomorrow lunchtime, I'm gonna chase you down and break your legs, understand?'

'If you break my legs' James said, remembering Mr Smith's advice, 'I imagine you'll be expelled from the school. Which also means you'll be expelled from the challenge. Which would then mean, I'd win.' He braced himself for a kick in the back of the head, which, surprisingly never came.

Instead, the huge square-headed child prodded his chest.

'Not if I make it look like a foul.'

James shivered. Maybe he wasn't lying.

'Oh' he added, 'what's that in your eye?'

James blinked, confused. Shane kicked sand in his face and stomped away, roaring with laughter.

Chapter 47

Having picked out most of the sand from his face and hair, James arrived home and dropped his rucksack in the usual place next to the sofa. He fully expected Auntie Sue to tell him he was late but, wait. Where was she? Not on the sofa. Not in the front room. It didn't smell of stale sweat in there. And the windows were open. Very strange. She must have been in the toilet. Or in bed. There was absolutely no way she'd be in the kitchen. No way whatso…

There she was. In the kitchen, chopping carrots and singing along to a song on the radio.

'Er, auntie?' He stuttered.

She spun round like a rhino on roller skates. 'What?!'

'Erm.'

'Stop stuttering!'

'It's just.'

'What? Never seen a woman dance while cooking dinner before?'

'Erm, I don't think so. What is it?' he said, peering into the bubbling pot on the hob.

'Summink healthy. You're getting under my feet. Ain't you got sumink else to do?' She snapped, waving a hot ladle in the air.

'Erm.'

'Practise for your...' she flapped a hand at the garden, '...challenge?'

'Yes. Yes. But. If I go into the back garden, won't you be able to see me?'

She flicked at a newly erected curtain by the back door. 'I can shut this.'

Picking up an old tennis ball, thrown over accidentally by the neighbours, he played a match against himself: England v Scotland at Wembley. He didn't know why or how he made this decision. Then, as the 'match' began, he did another strange thing; he started commentating on the game as though he'd been doing this kind of thing his whole life.

'And Dalglish passes to McCallister. Scotland have started strongly. McCallister plays a long ball forward to McGinn but that's well cut out by Gascoigne. Now Gascoigne for England. He beats one, he beats two, he plays a one two with Sterling and its Gascoigne! One nil to England!'

How did he know the names of these players? Who were these men? But his body didn't give him time to think. To celebrate the goal, scored between two rosemary bushes, James fell on his back with his arms outstretched and pretended to have water sprayed over his face. 'What the...?' But as he lay on the grass, staring up at the grey sky, another song began playing in his head. 'Three Lions', by Baddiel, Skinner and The Lightening Seeds.

Tears began welling in his eyes. What was going on? This song, how did he know it? What was it? And why was it making him feel so emotional? 'Three Lions' was England's big song at the Euro '96 tournament that Dad often talked about. Shearer, Sheringham, Gazza, and Southgate's penalty miss. All those brilliant England players. It was the year he met Mum and they went to some concerts, and it was the best summer ever and whenever dad scored a good goal he'd always copy Gazza's celebration after scoring against Scotland in that tournament.

Chapter 48

'James, you'll be on Margot's team. And er, just, do your best.' said Mr Smith, clearly not holding out much hope for the newcomer. The St Mark's Year Six school football team and trialists were huddled by the foot of the bank near the centre touchline listening intently to their coach.

Over the last two days, Margot had trained, coached, shouted and praised him as James worked his socks off in preparation for today's final session. It was amazing how much his body had remembered. He nodded nervously and slipped a yellow bib over Margot's old Partick top. Knowing this was his only chance to shine, he knew he must keep a check on his nerves; easier said than done. His legs felt heavy and stiff like they needed oiling.

It was a cloudy, moist afternoon. A day where the rain had threatened half-heartedly but decided it couldn't be bothered with the hassle. James scanned across the vastness of the deserted pitch and gulped a very dry gulp. Although exciting, it was also a foreboding sight, like a battlefield before the battle. Brand new '*Measure the Treasure*' nets, supplied by Brett Splatter, were hooked up around the freshly painted goals and Mr Smith had promised to also remark the pitch. It was beginning to look like a mini Wembley.

'Ok, let's get warmed up' shouted Mr Smith with a clap.

The players fanned out into two teams, bibs to the right, colours (basically kids not in bibs) to the left. James' team contained Margot, Banksy and Omar. Shane was captain of the opposition. Showing off slightly, Mr Smith juggled the ball with his feet to the centre circle before laying it to rest on the centre spot. James rubbed his legs, anxiously. Margot jogged across and held out a hair band.

'I forgot to give you this' she said.

'What is it?'

'You tie your hair back with it.'

James frowned, 'I'm not a girl.'

'Neither is Jack Grealish, but he wears one. It'll keep your hair out of your eyes.' Margot scraped his hair back and within seconds he had peripheral vision. 'Now, keep your head up when you've got the ball, ok?' James nodded. 'And look to play it in front of me so I can run onto it.' He nodded again, still fiddling with his new hairstyle. For a little while his face felt strange; like someone had pulled all his skin back. 'And maybe Shane won't recognise me?' he said, hopefully.

But Shane did. 'FA CUP LOOKS LIKE A GIRL!!!'

'ENOUGH!' barked Mr Smith. 'Let's play!'

Chapter 49

He blew the whistle and the Buzzcut brothers kicked off for Shane's colours. The game descended into a midfield scrum, with all tactics being blown away on the warm breeze. James was getting bored. For the first five minutes or so he didn't touch the ball. Neither had either goalie, but then the ball ran free on the left. He took a solid touch forward and dribbled up field towards the colours' goal.

'James! Through ball!' hollered Margot, sprinting past him at breakneck speed. She was so fast. Panicking slightly, he played it forward. More by luck than judgement, the ball was weighted perfectly for her to run onto. Margot knocked it past the onrushing keeper and slotted it into the empty goal at the near post.

1-0.

'Great pass, James!' grinned Margot, high-fiving him.

As he jogged back for the restart, he couldn't help but smile. He'd set up a goal with his first few touches. His confidence soared. A few minutes later, he picked up the loose ball and sprinted into the empty space ahead. Perhaps they left it free because they didn't think he'd be a threat? Whatever the reason, James took full advantage.

'*Get your head up. Look for the runners.*' he heard Dad shout in his head. This time he spotted Omar on the charge, flying in from the right. Only Shane and the keeper stood in their way.

'It's alright,' said Shane, 'It's only 'Fleurbler'. I've got him.'

James knew his nemesis would attack him at any given opportunity, so he laid the ball square to Omar, who made no mistake, firing a lovely first-time effort past the onrushing keeper, Ali.

2-0.

James peered across to Mr Smith, who gave him an approving thumbs up. It was all the endorsement the boy needed.

'Sick pass, FA Cup.' said Omar jumping on his back. 'But aren't you allergic to football?'

James smiled. 'Don't think I'd be playing if I was, Omar.'

'Keep your eye on Shane. He's out to get you.' said Margot.

With moments of the first half remaining, Omar knocked the ball out to James on the left wing. Shane began his charge. As he slid in, studs winking, James chipped the ball and hurdled over him in one swift move, but Shane caught his trailing ankle with a scything hack, and he clattered to the floor.

'That's just the start,' snarled Shane.

'Send him off, sir,' appealed Margot.

'He's going in too hard!' said Omar.

'It's ok' said James, hobbling to his feet. 'I can take it. Oi, Shane!' he called, shaking his bruised leg. 'Is that all you've got?'

He didn't know why he said this. He knew he was only causing more trouble for himself. Maybe it was because he thought he was in a safe environment. With Mr Smith watching over, he knew Shane couldn't beat him up. He was also feeling more confident. He was enjoying playing football again. He felt free and good and fit. Even his brain was helping now, conjuring up tips and tricks. He also knew this was his last chance to get in the team, and if he could really annoy Shane, the giant might lose the plot and get sent off. It was a dangerous strategy because the very next time he got the ball, Shane sent him flying with a shoulder barge. The boy mountain was definitely telling the truth about wanting to break his legs.

WALLOP! He hacked James down after an attempted nutmeg.

DOOF! Shane elbowed him in the ear as they went up for a header.

It was like watching a pussy cat being attacked by a lion.

'It's almost full time. Why don't you take a break?' said Margot. He'd just won a free kick on the edge of the area. Mr Smith rushed across the pitch to confront Shane. Both were making gestures with their arms.

'Any more fouls and you're off!'

'But I got the ball, sir.'

'The only time you've got the ball today, is on the centre spot when you kicked off.'

'He's cheating!'

'This is your final warning.'

Shane trudged away, kicking the turf in frustration.

'Have you worked out his weakness yet?' said Margot. James shook his head. 'Every opponent has one.'

'I've been trying to get him sent off.'

Margot grinned. 'What else?'

'He's quite slow.' He glanced down at his swollen legs. 'And he only kicks with his right foot.'

Margot smiled. 'Bingo! Shane can't use his left. He's completely one footed.'

Taking a short run up, Margot backheeled the ball. Shane was onto him in a flash, but this time James fainted left, took a touch to his right, and caught the defender off balance. The plan had worked. With the goal now gaping, he hit a low shot across Ali and into the far corner of the goal. A sudden surge of elation rushed through him like a bolt of lightning. He'd scored. James had scored a goal. A proper goal. In a net. And Shane was sat on grass, thumping the ground in frustration.

'HAAAAAAAAA!' he cried, punching the air as his jubilant teammates chased him.

Then Mr Smith blew the final whistle.

'The team-sheet for the final will be up on the noticeboard tomorrow lunchtime,' he shouted over the buzz in the dressing room. 'If you haven't made it into the squad, keep trying. And please, come and support us. We need all the help we can get.'

As he closed the changing room door, the teacher was surprised to see a familiar face waiting for him in the corridor.

'The kids are looking good for the final.' said Brett Splatter.

'What can I do for you?' said Mr Smith, trying his best to be polite.

'Mind if I have a quiet word?'

Chapter 50

His legs felt like sledgehammers. Upon inspection, both ankles were swollen and red raw. It was like he'd left them in a beehive for the night. He had an inch-long angry gash along his left calf and his shins were a bluey-red sunset. His knees were grazed, and his thighs pulsed with a dull thud. James hoped with all his heart it had been worth it. Today was the day he'd find out. The team sheet would be up after lunch. He blew out a nervous sigh and felt a stabbing pain in his stomach.

The sunny morning dragged on without end. Minutes took hours, hours took days. It was unbearable. His stomach had started hurting again, such was his fear of not being selected.

'What are you worrying about?' said Omar.

'You played great, James. Man-of-the-match performance,' said Margot.

Eventually, lunchtime arrived, and the hopefuls all waited in the corridor for Mr Smith to pin up the team. Shane sprinted towards, finishing with a knee slide, falling short of James by just a few centimetres.

'Dunno why you're waiting here.' he smirked. 'You ain't getting in the team.'

'Leave him alone Shane,' said Omar.

'Aye, leave him be.' said Margot.

'He's a wimp and I'm gonna break his legs,' threatened Shane.

'You keep saying that!' said Margot, jutting out her chin.

'You want some, Scotland?'

'Come on then,' goaded Margot, shoving him away.

In the middle of all this excitement, a song played in James' mind playlist, 'Saturday Night's All Right for Fighting' by Elton John. A rush of electricity coursed through him,

'Leave her alone, Lego head!'

The crowd burst out laughing. Shane's eyes darted around, confused and angry at their reaction. 'Protecting your girlfriend, are you?' he spat.

The two boys squared up to each other, the mismatch in height clear for all to see: shortest against tallest, heaviest against lightest.

'Break it up,' hollered Mr Smith rushing towards them. 'Come on, that's enough all of you.'

'It was James, sir, he was bullying me.'

'Enough' said Mr Smith, wearily. 'If I have to tell you off one more time, I'll drop you, not only from this team, but from this year.'

'You can't do that?' said Shane. 'My grandad runs this school!'

This comment seemed to enrage Mr Smith. He prodded a finger dangerously close to Shane's barrel chest and lowered his voice to almost a whisper.

'Your performance in class this year has been a disgrace. You haven't paid attention in one single lesson, and your grandad has repeatedly failed to listen to any of my concerns. Maybe you'll both start listening when I drop you down to Year Five next term.'

Shane's face went all blotchy and it looked for a moment that he might burst into tears. Mr Smith turned to the expectant group of hopefuls and with a cheery clap of the hands announced:

'Now, who wants to see the team sheet?'

There was a slight cheer as he stepped up to the noticeboard and pinned up the squad list. Standing in front of it, he explained:

'Remember, all those that haven't made the squad this time, don't give up. It was a very hard decision. Now, those selected listen carefully. The match is at two pm tomorrow and Mrs De'Ath has agreed to let you out of class at one fifteen to meet me in the dressing room. The rest of the school will be allowed watch too, so hopefully it'll be like Wembley Stadium out there. Any questions, come and find me. Otherwise, I'll see you tomorrow.'

He jogged away as the huddle of children surged towards the noticeboard. James was near the back. He didn't bother moving. Another few minutes wouldn't make much difference to the inevitable bad news anyway.

'Yes, I'm in,' said Omar.

Margot craned her neck, but Shane barged in front of

her. He followed his finger down the names until he could spell one.

'YESSSSSS!' he roared, in James' face. 'I'm off to win the World Cup.'.

The huddle finally thinned out and James stepped forward, head bowed. Margot, who was confirmed as captain, draped a sympathetic arm around him as he gazed down the list.

Chapter 51

JAKE BANKS (GK)
OMAR MINGO
SHANE SPLATTER
BROWN BUZZCUT
REKHA PATEL
MARGOT NAISMITH (C)
RYAN KIELY
BLONDE BUZZCUT
POLLY BACON
Subs:
HARVEY HARFORD
DANTE HILL
PIETR ANTIC

'Ah'm sorry James. I don't know what he's thinking' said Margot, sadly.

'S'ok.' James lied.

He wandered off alone to contemplate the bad news. It was over. The dream was done. He'd let his family down.

Now Shane Splatter would surely go on and win the trophy. The thought made him feel truly ill. He made his way outside to his favourite bit of wall on the outskirts of the playground to crumble and fold and mope and generally feel really sorry for himself.

The end of the school day was treated with a bigger cheer than usual which only made James feel worse.

'Who's up for a quick match in the new goals?' said Omar. 'Big practice before tomorrow's match?'

'Coming James?' teased Shane.

'Shut up!'

Margot loyally waited behind, but James knew she was eager to get out on the pitch, so he encouraged her to join the others.

'No. I'm staying with you.' She insisted.

As he gathered up his books, Mr Smith approached. 'I'm sorry I couldn't put you in the team, James.' Abject disappointment had numbed his tongue. 'I really wanted to.'

'Then why didn't you?'

Mr Smith drew in a deep breath. 'I didn't know you were still allergic to football.'

James felt winded. 'We've been through this. I told you it was a prank.'

'I was given a letter.'

'What letter?'

Mr Smith placed his allergy note on the table.

'But that's impossible' he cried. 'I tore it up!'

'This letter was clearly written by a doctor, and it clearly says you're allergic to football.'

'It's a fake! That doctor doesn't exist! You told me to watch out for liars. Well, this letter is a lie!'

'Who would do something like that?'

James fell silent. No matter how much he wanted to be in the team, he couldn't snitch on his auntie. Mr Smith shook his head, sadly.

'My hands are tied. I'm sorry James. What if you are allergic and it suddenly comes back during the final, and I can't help you? I'd be seriously putting your health at risk, and I can't afford to do that.'

Tears of frustration escaped down the boy's cheeks.

'This isn't fair.'

'Sorry James. I can't take that chance.'

Chapter 52

Instead of sulking and trudging out of the classroom huffing and puffing, James stormed out in a white-hot fury. One name was on his mind: Brett Splatter. Brett Splatter stealing Wills, taking his rucksack, becoming fake friends with Auntie Sue, putting Dad in prison. Brett Splatter had ruined his life.

Margot and Omar were waiting for him by the gates.

'You look like you're about to go into battle!' said Margot.

'I'm going to that liar, Brett Splatter's mansion, to get Wills back and find out how he framed Dad. Anyone up for it?'

'Shane's house? Yeah. I went a few months ago' said Omar. 'I know a good way in round the back. Just follow the orange footprints.'

James and Margot looked at each other.

'Nah, it's true. Listen…' He proceeded to explain that a few months ago, he'd been invited to Shane's for a FIFA sleepover. However, Shane insisted they go on an expedition to the mansion by starting their mission near the bottom of his enormous garden at the kebab shop on the High Street. After almost choking on a chicken donner, Shane, thinking he was being really clever, led them through the alley running alongside it and got his foot stuck a tin of orange paint. The rest of their journey was therefore documented by orange imprints of Shane's size nineteen feet.

'What's the plan?' said Margot, as they marched along the High Street.

Booming basslines blasted into the warm air from shuddering car windows, voices of all nationalities chattered eagerly as they squeezed past the bus queue.

'Just follow the orange paint.'

'Once we're inside!'

'I want Wills back and I want Brett Splatter to stop hating my family.'

As instructed by Omar, they crossed the road by Lidl and stopped outside the alleyway next to the kebab shop. The alley was dark and stank of three-day old farts. After deciding this was the correct alley, James stepped into it. The stench was shocking, almost as bad as Auntie Sue's armpits. Then something hard and possibly furry squelched beneath his feet. Moving forward a few more tentative steps, he skidded on something slippery. Was it a dead rat or human blood or some brains? Panicking, he rushed forwards and cluttered into a pile of loose paint tins. Was this where Shane had got his foot stuck?

After stumbling inelegantly past them he trod on a skewer of mouldy kebab meat and careered through a sticky spider web and out the other side into daylight. He brushed the cobwebs from his face, scraped the brains (or rat) from his trainers and found himself in an almost empty scrap yard.

'See the orange tracks?' said Margot, pointing to the dusty ground ahead.

'How did you do that?' said James, gaping at her.

'What?'

'Not get anything on you?'

She smiled, 'It was like zigzagging through a bunch of defenders.'

Following Shane's orange tracks, they scrambled through a rusty wire fence into a larger clearing of wasteland. Weeds had erupted from the cracks in the uneven concrete; nature was fighting back against its man-made enemy. Oil spillages, discarded bits of car engines and shards of glass added to the rough terrain. Up ahead loomed a ridiculously high brick wall. On closer inspection, the section directly in front of them was stained with smears of orange paint.

'That must be where Shane lost his temper for the first time.'

Margot was preoccupied, scouring the grass and weeds like a bloodhound, looking out for the slightest speck of orange on the leaves. Slowly, she followed the gentle curve of the wall. The undergrowth grew deeper and deeper. James stumbled clumsily behind, beating away huge great stinging nettles and prickly bushes with a stick.

'Ow!' he moaned. 'Stupid Stinging nettles!' Then, 'Margot? Where are you?' All he could see was green. 'Ow!'

'Here, James! Walk towards my voice.'

'How can I walk towards a voice?'

'Just listen out for the sound and when it gets louder you know you're close!' she hollered. James suddenly appeared.

'No need to shout' he smiled.

Margot was stood like a surfer on an old gnarly tree trunk resting at an inviting angle against the top of the wall. Two faded footsteps told them Shane must have climbed it.

After a few juddering slips, James followed his graceful friend up the trunk to the top. With a huge sigh of relief, he swung his legs over the wall and took in the scene ahead.

Stretched out before them were the sloping grounds of the Splatter mansion. Looking slowly up the hill he could see huge clumps of trees, long stretches of parkland scattered with lime coloured golf greens. High up at the top stood a dark, rectangular mansion, peering down on nature like a strict teacher. A smaller dark block stood out to the side, attracting a great deal of activity. Workers in dark clothes were unloading huge boxes from a line of trucks emblazoned with the 'Measure the Treasure' logo and disappearing through a wide opening into the house. There was also an obedient line of elderly people snaking along the perimeter, slowly being admitted through the opening.

'That must be the 'Measure the Treasure' studio' said James.

'Imagine having a TV studio in your house?'

'Do you think those people are going to watch a show?'

'Only one way to find out.'

She jumped down, beckoning James to join her. He looked down and felt woozy. The ground seemed to jump up at him.

'It's miles down there. You're loads bigger than me. You've got less distance to travel.'

Margot picked up some loose earth and threw it lightly at him.

'Stop!'

'I'll stop when you jump down.' She threw another clump, spattering his legs.

'Margot!'

After the third throw he let go and fell to the floor with a small thud.

'You got me in the mouth' he complained, spitting out earth.

The bracken crunched beneath them as they stealthily walked through the grounds, keeping to the beds along the left wall, weaving through the thickets and shrubs and ancient trees. As the house drew nearer, they began to hear chattering voices, crunching feet on gravel and the clanging sounds of metal. His heart raced. He needed to hold his nerve. What was he going to do? Search the house trying to avoid being seen? It was a huge house. Wills could be in any one of the fifty rooms inside.

They eventually reached the top and crouched down

on the gravel by a large greenhouse. There was no point looking for Shane's footprints anymore. The house was now only fifty yards ahead. Looking through the mildewed windows, he could see an obvious way in via a huge square opening through which groups of adults were heading. At the side of the house was a gravel driveway, where more people hopped off a coach towards the queue.

'Let's tag on the end' whispered James. Margot nodded.

CRUNCH! *Why is gravel so noisy?* He wondered. *Why isn't there a volume button so you can turn it down?* Straightening up alongside a cluster of chattering adults, they were ushered through a big wide-open space, along a black curtained walkway and up a scaffolding staircase. Banks of bright lights hung from the ceiling.

'Move along the aisle and take a seat' said a woman in a t-shirt with the word CREW on it.

Against his will, James shuffled to the end and looked out. He was inside a TV studio. As his row quickly filled up, he realised there was no escape from the inevitable. He was about to watch a live broadcast of 'Measure the Treasure'.

Chapter 53

'I've never seen a live TV show before' said Margot, excitedly.

'Seriously?!' said James. 'You're seriously looking forward to watching this...this...nightmare?!'

'Enjoy it,' smiled Margot. 'Also, he's gonna be busy. Maybe we can sneak into the house at the interval?'

The camera crew shuffled onto the set with the show's two on-screen experts; a well-suited gentleman with a monocle and an elegantly dressed lady dripping with a sparkling neck. Taking a bow, they sat down at a table marked EXPERTS. Then the first guest was shunted into position behind the opposite desk marked GUEST. Finally, Brett Splatter appeared, flanked by a bevy of fawning fusspots. As he crossed to the centre desk, he gave the audience a big wave, who responded with a huge cheer.

'Brett Splatter's definitely playing at home. He's got the whole crowd on his side' said Margot.

'He's probably paying them' said James.

'Silence on set.' Barked a slim lady with a blonde ponytail. Her black t-shirt read FLOOR MANAGER. 'We're live in five, four...'

Brett Splatter looked up at the centre camera and put on his most dazzling smile.

'And welcome to the first of two live World Cup specials of 'Measure the Treasure'.'

James and Margot gawped at each other.

'World Cup?' mouthed James.

The audience were encouraged to clap by a man lifting up a sign saying 'CLAP!' James didn't bother. Brett Splatter continued.

'We're here this evening in the studio, and tomorrow we'll be at a secret location where we have a bonzer surprise for you. But more of that later. First, let's welcome our two resident antiques experts...'

And so, it continued. Various guests were herded on to show their antiques and offer amusing stories about them. The experts then guessed the weight and value of the antiques, with the closest estimate earning the guest ten points. Blah. It was deathly boring. Tonight's show was slightly more interesting because all the antiques (trinkets) were from World Cup tournaments. An old lady brought on a ball apparently used in the 1982 tournament in Spain. Although in truth it looked like any tatty ball one might find in a shed. A man wearing an eye patch then came on with one of Maradona's shin pads, claiming he wore it in 1994. But again, having not been signed by the player, it looked like he might have brought it from a boot sale for 10p. With the hot lights beaming down and the dull tone of the host's voice, James felt his eyelids grow heavy, and eventually he nodded off, resting his head on Margot's shoulder.

'My final guest tonight,' Brett Splatter announced, 'is a lady who has kept an incredible piece of treasure under her bed for years, completely unaware of its worth.'

A gasp went up from the audience.

'I know. So many of us have no idea what's under our noses, do we?'

He paused.

'I've left this 'til last because it's a warmup for tomorrow's spectacular unveiling. Ladies and gentlemen, please give a warm welcome to the lovely Sue Eligus!'

James woke with a start, which made Margot almost jump out of her seat.

'Is that your auntie?' she said.

The audience clapped noisily as Auntie Sue waddled onto the set wearing a face mask and gloves. James leaned forward in disbelief.

Brett Splatter looked surprised at her appearance.

'So, er, Sue.' He whispered in her ear. 'What's with the mask and gloves?'

'Allergy to fleurbler' she announced.

He leaned in and whispered, 'You never wore this in rehearsal.'

'You never told me I'd have to pretend to own something to do with fleurbler' she said.

He straightened up and gave her his trademark, professional grin.

'So, what have you got for us then, Suzy Sue?'

Above the audience hung two large TV monitors

showing the action as it happened.

Auntie Sue's masked face filled the screen.

'It's a stupid little furry lion' she sneezed.

'Sorry?' he said, through gritted teeth.

'I dunno' she shrugged. 'You gave me it. But I do remember my nephew had one just like this when he was younger.'

Brett Splatter did his best to hide his agitation. He turned to a camera.

'This, ladies and gentlemen, is the official mascot of the 1966 World Cup. His name is World Cup Willy.'

Auntie Sue sneezed into her mask. Brett Splatter curled his lip in frustration.

'Isn't it adorable?' he said, taking it from her.

High in the audience, James sat up, eyes burning with fury.

'Here's the great surprise' continued the host. 'Inside World Cup Willy is something even more special. Something I don't think anyone knows about.'

Brett Splatter turned the lion round so the audience could see its back. Taking a small knife from his jacket pocket, he cut a slit between the legs and squeezed its tummy. From its foamy innards, a tiny gold coin, the size of a 5p piece, dropped out of its bottom and into his hand. The audience clapped. James stood up and shouted,

'THAT'S MINE!'

'Sit down!' said a man sitting behind him.

The host held the coin close to the camera. Engraved

on the face was the outline of the Jules Rimet trophy, while curled around the edge were the words:

WORLD CUP 1966   No 5 of 5   24 CARAT GOLD

'As you can see ladies and gentlemen, this is a special commemorative World Cup 1966 coin. Very rare, very gold and extremely sought after.'

Brett Splatter oozed across the stage and passed the lion and coin to the experts.

'They both look like authentic pieces from 1966.' The lady in gold gleamed. 'The Football Association only made five of these coins, making it very valuable. It's also solid gold.'

Auntie Sue sneezed again.

Monocle man also held it up to his glassy eye.

'Extraordinary!' he gasped, 'and the gold looks like turn-of-the-century French. Possibly from the same batch that made the Jules Rimet Trophy.'

Another sneeze. This time Brett Splatter turned his head and gave her a filthy glare, before beaming back into the camera.

'You're both right!' – the audience applauded – 'World Cup Willy was England's mascot for the 1966 World Cup finals. But this one is extra special. Because of the coin, there are only one or two of these left in the world.'

Auntie Sue tottered unsteadily.

'That would raise the value significantly' said monocle man.

Brett Splatter stepped to the front of the stage and held his hands out.

'Now, ladies and gentlemen, what do you think both these items are worth? Are you ready to…'?

The audience shouted out '**Measure the Treasure!**'

Gold lady estimated the mascot's weight at fifty grammes, and the coin five grammes with a value of £10,000. James and Margot gawped at each other. Monocle man thought the mascot weighed seventy grammes, the coin eight grammes with a combined value of £15,000.

'The actual weight of the lion is…'

There followed a dramatic drum roll.

'Fifty-two grammes. So well done to Dame Goldie. The coin weighs nine grammes, so Lord Monocle, you win that one. And their combined value…'

There was a dramatic pause. Brett Splatter wiped his brow with a hankie. James leaned forward in his seat, unsure whether he hated Brett Splatter or Auntie Sue more.

'You'll never believe this, folks… World Cup Willy and the gold coin are worth £50,000!'

The audience gasped in astonishment.

James cried out 'THAT BELONGS TO ME!'

And Auntie Sue fainted.

Chapter 54

Wills was worth FIFTY THOUSAND POUNDS. FIFTY THOUSAND POUNDS! Auntie Sue was on the floor. His mind was in a spin. Her allergy. She needed help, quickly. FIFTY THOUSAND POUNDS! How had Brett Splatter known there was a coin inside Wills? He cast his thoughts back to the photo of grandad with the men from the FA when he was ten. Wills in one hand and a little coin in the other. They were his prizes for finding the trophy.

Back on stage, with the cameras still rolling, Brett Splatter was struggling to come to terms with a guest who had dared to faint on his show and a boy who dared shout out. James sensed an opportunity and got Margot to start recording the events on her phone. The outraged host marched across the stage to Auntie Sue. 'Seriously?' He said. 'You faint over a tiddly little fifty grand? It's nothing!'

'Allergy.' She croaked.

He pushed away her outstretched hand. 'You did this on purpose you silly fat tub of lard. Coming on with a mask and gloves. You've just done this to humiliate me!'

'She needs help.' said Lady Gold, rushing over.

'Epi-Pen.' Said Auntie Sue, pointing vaguely to her shoe. Lady Gold acted quickly, jabbing the needle into her flabby arm.

'She's fine.' Said the host. 'No-one's allergic to football. I gave her the idea to make her nephew believe he was allergic to it.'

James gasped. 'I KNEW IT!'

'You called me fat.' Said Auntie Sue, sitting up slowly.

'Well, you are.' The audience gasped. 'Now, tell me the passcode for the Nerve Centre!'

'Will you jolly well leave her alone.' Said Lady Gold.

'Will you jolly well leave her alone.' he mocked with a high-pitched poshness. 'You Pom's* think you're better than the rest of us, don't you! With your fancy Royals and your stupid little teacups and your precious 1966 World Cup win that you go on about every flaming day.' He waved the floor manager away with a firm hand. 'Well, I'll show you lot. Tomorrow, your precious little Jules Rimet trophy will be mine, all mine! And then I'll be the most famous person in the world, and I can say goodbye to this awful show and you awful people!'

The floor manager tapped the host on the shoulder and whispered in his ear. 'We're still live, Mr Splatter. I think some people might have heard what you just said.'

'Well, turn the bloody CAMERA'S OFF!' The camera operators shook their heads, slowly. Brett Splatter froze. Feeling the blood drain from his face, he gazed out to the disgusted looking audience. 'Oh.' He spluttered. 'Er, hahahahahaha. I was only messing about.' He turned to Auntie Sue, desperately. 'Wasn't I.'

She shook her head in disgust. 'I used to love your

show, and I used to love you. But my nephew was right. You're a thief and a liar. I only came on here to see what it was like being on telly. After this, I'll never watch your stupid show ever again.'

The audience stood up and cheered loudly. Brett Splatter looked lost and bewildered. He mopped his sweaty brow and laughed nervously. 'She's such a funny actress.' He was about to continue his appeal when the floor manager strode confidently in front of him and bellowed... 'And we're off air in 5-4'

'But!' squeaked Brett Splatter.

'2-1...'

The theme tune blared across the studio.

'Guessing your bounty
Is such a pleasure
So please join us on 'Measure the Treasure'!'

Chapter 55

The audience were hurried out of their seats.

'Move along quickly.' fussed the floor manager as James and Margot hurried down to join Auntie Sue.

As the seats emptied, Brett Splatter re-appeared, white with rage.

'I thought I heard you whining, Eligus!'

'Where's Wills?' cried James.

'Safely out of your reach.'

Gripping each child by the wrist, he turned to Auntie Sue with a sneer. 'You lot, come with me!'

'No!'

'I don't want my boys to use force on you, just yet.'

Les and Brian appeared behind him, flexing their muscles. James gulped and stopped struggling.

They were led through a blue door, then along a stone floored corridor and into the grand entrance of the main building. Huge portraits of Brett Splatter adorned the walls. In one picture, he was stood on the shoulders of Australian football teammates, proudly lifting the Jules Rimet trophy. There was also a giant black and white print of a young boy with a chubby face holding up the trophy.

James confronted the game show host.

'Why do you hate my family so much? Why have you tried to ruin my life?'

The old man grinned and pointed to the black and white print.

'That's me when I was ten years old. My father had just taken the trophy. Well, he stole it from a display, but I like to say he liberated it. The year was 1966. We were a poor family but selling the trophy would make us rich. He found a buyer, but then your grandfather, snooping around the park on his bloody roller skates, messed everything up!'

'He did the right thing!'

'Not for us. We had to leave the country because the police were chasing us! As I sat on the plane to Australia, I made a promise to myself, that one day I would be the owner of the trophy. I got close, so many times, but who always stood in my way? Your blasted grandfather! Then your dad. Now you. But that's all about to change, because tomorrow, the trophy will be all mine!'

Just then, the floor manager approached with Wills and the little gold coin. Putting them swiftly in his pocket, Brett Splatter took her to one side.

'Were the microphones on at the end?' She nodded; he clutched his head. 'Get me the viewing figures. I need to know how many people heard me.'

Both Brian and Les seemed distracted by the hushed conversation.

Seizing the opportunity, James kicked Les in the shin. 'OWWW!'

Wasting no time, Margot stamped on Brian's foot.

'You little…!'

'Quick' said James. 'Through the corridor!'

'What about me?' cried Auntie Sue.

'Stay there. Sit down. We'll be back soon!'

The floors were made of polished stone. Heavy wooden doors stood either side of the green painted walls. It was an imposing and dark house.

'What's the plan?' panted Margot.

'Dunno. Stay alive?'

With Les and Brian hobbling after them, they reached the end of the corridor and skidded to their left, finding themselves in a huge kitchen with no exit doors.

'No good' puffed James turning back, 'go the other way.'

This corridor led them directly into a huge barn with oak beams, a long, soft sofa and the square-headed Shane, who was consumed by a shooting game on a giant projector screen. In the far corner, next to a dusty fireplace was another door, and it was open. They hurdled over the sofa and made a charge for it.

'Alright Shane?' said Margot, without looking back. 'Don't get up.'

Shane Splatter lurched forwards.

'Scotland!' he boomed. 'FA CUP!'

The panting duo scrambled through the door and raced up five flights of stairs to the very top floor. With legs burning they hurried along the corridor pushing down on the door handles.

'In here, quick' hissed James, opening the first door with a creak.

'Too obvious. Keep going!'

Every other door was locked except the one right at the end, which Margot flung open. With a solid thumbs up, James followed her inside the dark room and gently closed the door.

Just moments later, Shane and Brian began rattling those same doors.

'Mister Splatter's never let me up here before' said Brian

'I know why' said Shane.

'Is it because his bedroom's smelly?'

'He's got a secret room full of old junk he calls 'treasure''

Just as Shane was about to push down on the door James and Margot were hiding behind, he heard a commotion coming from downstairs.

'That must be them!' he cried.

'Quick' said Brian.

They thudded off, stomping down the stairs two at a time.

Margot clutched her chest with relief as James felt for a light switch and flicked it on. Before them was a room full of junk; in other words, they'd found themselves inside Brett Splatter's treasure room.

'It stinks of moths and Auntie Sue's wardrobe!' said James, stepping over a cluster of golf clubs.

'It's like the charity shop my Nana worked in' said Margot, pushing past a rail of clothes. 'What shall we do, hide in here for as long as poss?

James took a floppy hat from a mannequin and put it on.

'Let's pretend we're lost old ladies. Say Auntie Sue is our helper and leg it!'

Margot laughed. James went over to the fireplace and lifted the digger on the tractor toy.

'I mean, why does he have all this old junk?'

Suddenly, the wall began to move outwards at an angle, forcing James to step back in alarm.

'You've opened a secret door! I've always wanted to go through a secret door!' cried Margot.

James slid through the gap and looked inside.

'Margot' he whispered, 'you'd better come a see this!'

Sat on a small shelf, lit up with a single spotlight, was a gold cup that looked very much like the Jules Rimet trophy.

Chapter 56

They stood in silence, gawping at the trophy.

'Is it real?' said James.

Margot shrugged. What if the challenge was set up by Brett Splatter? He hit the heel of his hand against his head.

'I'm so gullible! I fell for it completely. He's had the World Cup all along.'

Margot frowned. 'Don't be daft. This can't be the real Jules Rimet trophy. It's Brett Splatter we're talking about. Not even his tan's real!'

Suddenly the treasure room door swung open, and Brett Splatter appeared, with Shane hovering over his shoulder.

'Welcome to my secret treasure room, kids!' He turned to Shane. 'I've got this from here, Shaney. Off you pop back downstairs, there's a love.'

'No. I'm staying to finish off these two.'

'You couldn't finish a bag of chips. Let me handle this.'

Shane stuck out his chin. 'Why did you say on telly just now that the trophy was gonna be yours?'

'Did I?' said the old man, straightening his tie. 'My tongue must have slipped. I often say things on TV I don't mean.'

'You said you made this challenge for me.'

The presenter took a deep breath.

'Go downstairs, or I'll ban you from video games for a month.'

With a giant huff, Shane turned his back and trudged off down the many stairs. With a cunning grin, the old man strode to the secret door and pushed it fully open as James and Margot stepped aside.

'Let me tell you what's going to happen.' he announced. 'First, I'm going to explain a few things, then you're going to enjoy a lovely night in the guest bedroom. There's no bed, unfortunately, and its stiflingly hot at night. Apart from that you'll have a comfy night's kip. And if you're good little children, I'll set you free just after the final whistle blows on our cup final tomorrow. How's that?'

'Against the law' said James. 'And that's not the real trophy.' he bluffed, pointing at it.

'No, but it was real enough to convince your father.'

James' eyes widened. The very thought of being in the same room that his dad was tricked sent a shiver down the small boy's back. His mind raced, trying to connect the dots. So, Brett Splatter must have used the fake trophy to lead Dad into this room. The one remaining question was, how was Dad caught with jewellery in his pockets?

'Why don't you take a look? This was the replica given to the England team soon after the final. It's still very valuable.'

James looked at him, then the trophy, then back at the old man. What harm could it do, to hold the replica?

He took a closer look at the trophy. It was very shiny and inviting. He raised a hand and touched the goddess Nike's feet. He squeezed his hand around her ankles and was about to lift the trophy when a shiver ran through him. On the underside of the shelf, he spotted the end of a tiny clear tube. He followed it along the shelf and down the corner of the wall, where it was attached to a cannister with the words 'SLEEPING GAS' printed across the front.

So that was how Dad was caught; he was lured to the trophy, picked it up and knocked out with sleeping gas. While he was asleep on the floor, Splatter must have stuffed his pockets with jewellery, then called the police. But James wasn't as gullible.

'No, I think I'll leave it' he said, watching the host's face screw up with frustration.

Margot subtly waved her phone at him, giving James an idea.

'Have you checked YouTube recently?'

It seemed to catch the old man off balance.

'What do you mean?'

'Just wondered if anyone had posted tonight's show? It was a really good episode.'

Brett Splatter rummaged around his jacket pocket in the tight space; tossing out bits of paper, credit cards, keys, World Cup Willy and the gold coin until he found it. Moments later, the host's complexion went very pale. A remix of his finest moments, looped together under a dance music beat had amassed almost two million views.

Your precious World Cup will be all mine
It's an awful show
You awful English

James could see the panic in the old man's eyes. His ego had been well and truly crushed. This was James' big chance. Now to finish him off.

'Do you love that trophy up there, Mr Splatter?'

'Yes.' he hissed, glaring at his phone.

'Well, you took three things from me that I loved most in the world: my dad, football and my little toy lion.

'Diddums.'

'So now, I'm gonna take something of yours. Cover your face, Margot!'

In a flash, he pushed past the old man and pretended to make a grab for the trophy. In reality, he deliberately gave it the slightest of nudges, just enough to activate the sensor. Outraged, the old man dropped his phone and threw him backwards.

'No-one touches my little Julie.' he said, correcting its position. The two kids hurried out into the treasure room, as an invisible plume of smoke wafted into his face.

'No!'

He drew back, panicking, rubbing his cheeks. He turned to the kids.

'You little…!'

The old man fell to his knees and accidentally coughed out his false teeth before sprawling, face down on the carpet and falling into a deep sleep.

Silence.

'Is he alright?' said Margot, prodding him.

The bald man suddenly let out a rip-roaring snore.

'Sleeping gas' said James, grinning.

'You did it!' shrieked Margot, giving him a little hug.

'Not a bad plan, eh? He might be awake in a few minutes, so let's grab Wills and Auntie Sue and get out of this dump!'

Chapter 57

The corridor was empty. The faint sound of a TV newscaster could be heard downstairs. And voices, male voices. They crept down the stairs and tiptoed along the stone corridor. Brian, Les and Shane were playing cards on the kitchen table next to Auntie Sue, whose head was buried sadly in her arms. A TV showing twenty-four-hour news played on the far wall. Carefully, James peeked through a gap in the door just in time to see Auntie Sue to lift her head and ask,

'When are you going to let me go?'

Without looking up from his cards, Les answered.

'After Mr Splatter's won his World Cup back.'

Shane looked up, shocked.

'What did you say?'

'After Mr Splatter's won his World Cup back.'

Shane was gobsmacked. 'His World Cup? HIS WORLD CUP?!' He stood up, sending the cards across the table. Les and Barry looked at each other.

'Calm down, Shaney.'

'You calm down! Who's done all the work for this cup?'

'You have, Shaney.'

'And who was the one who got invited to the challenge?'

'You were, Shaney.'

Shane nodded. 'And who's the one who gonna keep the Jules Rimet trophy after I win it tomorrow?'

'Mr Splatter is' said Brian, without thinking.

'No, Brian,' he pointed to himself. 'Me. I'm keeping it, not him.'

'But he said…'

'I don't care what he said, Les.'

As the argument escalated, James saw his opportunity to rescue his beleaguered auntie. To grab her attention, he pushed Wills through the gap in the door and wiggled the toy from side to side. Her eyes lit up as the small boy gestured with the lion's arm to join them. Gently, she slid her chair backwards and sneaked across the kitchen floor towards them. Just as she pulled the door closed behind her, Brett Splatter's name was announced by the newscaster. An immediate silence took hold. Then, as his name was mentioned again, Shane, Les and Brian wandered, like mystified zombies, away from the table towards the TV.

'We're just hearing that Australian game show host, Brett Splatter, has lashed out at one of his guests for fainting on his show 'Measure the Treasure' earlier this evening. In a harsh rant at one of his guests, Brett Splatter appeared to make sizeist remarks and admitted his show was dreadful…'

From the other side of the door, Margot and James shared a fist bump, while Auntie Sue pointed along the corridor whispering:

'Let's get moving!'

Stealthily and silently, they hurried back through the long corridors to the blue door where the house ended, and the studio began.

Efficiently, the TV crew bustled around pushing huge black boxes from the studio towards the vast opening outside, paying no attention whatsoever to the escaping trio. But then, just as they were about to set foot on the shingles and see the light of the moon, the floor manager shouted after them.

'Ignore her' puffed James, refusing to look back.

'Excuse me!' cried the floor manager, and, before they knew it, she had raced ahead and stopped them with a firm hand.

In desperation, James began his appeal.

'I'm sorry, but your boss is a lying thief.' He held up Wills to illustrate his point. 'He stole my toy, put my dad in prison and made Auntie Sue cry.'

The young woman nodded.

'He is, and I've just quit. Do you need any help?'

He glanced over his shoulder.

'Shane and those two big blokes are chasing us.' Right on cue, the blue door swung open and out spilled Les, Brain and Shane, looking very cross indeed.

The young woman pulled a car key from her pocket and handed it to Auntie Sue.

'I'll stall them. You get my car started and wait. It's the red sports car on the front row of the lawn.'

It was now dark outside. Van lights illuminated the

slow-moving cars making their way down the long drive. James and Margot raced to the car and watched anxiously as Auntie Sue appeared from the corner of the mansion and waddled across the gravel towards them. A few seconds later - followed by the arm-waving floor manager – Les, Brian and Shane came into view, making rapid ground on the big woman.

'They're catching you!' cried James, his fingernails digging nervously on the plastic dashboard.

'FA CUP!' roared Shane, pointing at his arch enemy.

It was a straight race to the red car, the puffing slug versus the panting rhinos. For some reason, it reminded James of a sack race at sports day; a slow race with lots of effort. Miraculously, Auntie Sue edged in first, slapping the bonnet with sweaty fingers. Hearing the men right behind her, she spun round to face them with her hands in the air.

'Listen, you've got us. We'll come clean.'

'Alright, but no funny stuff' said Brian.

'As if! Look at me!' She said, glancing down at her bouncy frame. 'I'm twenty-four stone and I haven't run since 1991.'

Les grinned.

'Okay put your hands in front of you'.

'Big mistake' she murmured.

Grabbing a fistful of jacket with both hands, she kicked the side of his leg and swept his balance clean away. Keeping close hold, she pushed her weight forward and landed on top of him like she was trying out a new mattress.

THUD!

Sensing the advancing threat of Brian, she pushed up onto her elbows, spun her feet round and kicked his ankles sending him crashing down beside her. With an almighty heave, she scrambled across the grass, twisted his neck and held him in a vice-like headlock.

The kids in the car looked on, amazed.

'Auntie, how did you do that?'

'Judo' she grinned. 'I was the British junior champion. Your grandad got me into it when I was about your age. Now I know why. To keep me away from Fleurbler.'

James grinned to himself. *Jubo is judo*! he smiled to himself. *The box under her bed that was next to mine. JUBO.*

Auntie Sue loomed over Les like a bear looking down at its dinner. He was terrified.

'Had enough, big boy?' she asked him.

Unable to move his head, he tapped the grass to submit. The big woman let go and clambered to her feet. She wiped her brow and surveyed her groaning victims. Next in her sight was Shane, who held up his hands in surrender and backed away towards the house.

'And don't even consider going for more help. We won't be as gentle next time!' She shouted, before squeezing into the driver's seat and revving the engine.

Chapter 58

Brushing away the matted curls, James woke the following morning, the morning of the cup final, with a great big smile on his face. Brett Splatter, the man who had single-handedly demolished his happiness had been defeated, at least for the time being. James hadn't fallen for his trap. Maybe he wasn't so gullible after all. The tiny ten-year-old had equalised for the Eligus family. The big question now was, could he find a winner?

During the drive home last night, Auntie Sue had stopped the car and burst into apologetic tears. She hugged James for ages, sobbing 'I'm so sorry!' onto his head, which was nice but made his hair sticky and wet. It was pretty cringy knowing Margot and the floor manager were watching too, but when he looked back, she too was sniffing back the tears. Auntie Sue also promised to call Mr Smith and tell him she'd made up his allergy. Pretty brave stuff, even though she should never have lied to him. And she most definitely should never have listened to the Australian celebrity. But he felt he had to forgive her; after all, she was the only family he had who wasn't in gaol.

It was the final day of the school year and everyone, including the teachers, were in high spirits. The children arrived excitedly in dresses, football kits, t-shirts and jeans; all except James, who had forgotten it was a non-uniform day.

During registration, Mr Smith gave a little speech thanking them all for being, on the whole, good students. He wished them well in high school and urged them to live up to their potential. He then urged the class to support the team in their quest to win their first ever cup final. A big cheer went up. He added that there had been an interesting development regarding one of his students who was eager to play and called James to his desk.

'Auntie Sue called me this morning and we've been in touch with your doctors. They've assured me that you're not allergic to football. So, would you like to be one of the subs for today's match?'

James nodded, his eyes huge like a kitten.

'Yes please!'

Mr Smith chuckled and patted him on the back.

'I have an announcement to make.' He called, drawing a hush. 'In case any of you thought otherwise, let me just clarify this; James Eligus is not allergic to football, so I've added him to the squad for today's big match.'

While the kids whooped and hollered, James caught the eye of Shane, who was sulking silently at the back. He glared back fiercely but his eyes seemed to have lost that terrifying glint that James was so used to. The huge boy continued to sulk silently all morning and at break time, instead of smashing footballs into gardens and picking fights, he sat gloomily on James' favourite bit of wall.

Chapter 59

Before lunch, the 'Measure the Treasure' vans started pulling up and unloading their kit on the playground. Brett Splatter had organised a special live 'roadshow' episode, to promote the area and St Mark's school. That's what he told Mrs De'Ath anyway. In truth, he was expecting Shane to win the cup so he could exclusively reveal it to the world, creating a media storm, which would make him super famous.

However, he hadn't been seen all morning. He'd disappeared out of sight. His phone was off, he wasn't at home, he couldn't be found in his studio or at the school. The producers bit their fingernails, the new floor manager lost her voice and all of them were certain he'd been scared away by the morning's news headlines:

'THE GREAT GAME SHOW MELTDOWN!'
'SPLAT GOES HIS CAREER!'
'SPLATTER THE SIZEIST SWINDLER!'

At 1.30, those players involved in the cup final were taken out of class and marched eagerly to the dressing rooms. With Brett Splatter still at large, the TV producers decided to scrap filming 'Measure the Treasure' and decided to broadcast the school cup final in the hope the trophy may still make a miraculous appearance. Also, as the timeslot had been booked and paid for, the football offered them something to film; and after Splatter's outburst last night, they'd all be looking for new jobs on Monday anyway.

The pitch looked perfect; Mr Smith had got in early to re-chalk the markings and roll out the famous Wembley stripes on the lush green turf. The new 'Measure the Treasure' nets wafted gently behind freshly painted white goalposts. Top football pundit Clive Spillesly had even been called in to commentate from a specially made gantry, and there seemed to be cameras everywhere.

During lunch play, with pretty much the whole school buzzing around the 'Measure the Treasure' trailers and staging, James spotted Shane sat on the wall at the back of the playground wearing a troubled expression.

He wasn't sure why, but James felt a bit sorry for him. Maybe it was because he'd spent so long sat there himself and knew how Shane might be feeling? He frowned, doubtfully. Shane wasn't scared of anything or anyone. They were also about to do battle against one another, like gladiators, only on the same team, with a football and not bone shattering sceptres. So, why did he find himself wandering up to his opponent; this awful, horrible, malicious bully who had made his life a living hell? Again, he had no idea.

'Alright Shane?'

'Get lost, FA Cup.'

James twitched. That ridiculous nickname had annoyed him for yonks.

'Why do you call me that?'

Shane mockingly put his fingers in his ears and stuck his elbows out.

The small boy shook his long locks. 'Not anymore.'

The beast snorted.

'Nervous about the match?'

'Stop trying to be my friend.'

'I just wanted to say good luck.'

'Like I'm gonna need it against you.'

James puffed out his cheeks. At least he'd tried. He turned on his heels to leave.

'I'm gonna shoot every time I get the ball' shouted Shane.

'Good plan.'

'Then I'm gonna throw you off the scaffolding and break your legs.'

This was most certainly a lie.

'See you in the dressing room.'

'FA Cup, fleurbler loser!'

At 1.45 the kids of St Mark's started boisterously filling the bank along the touchline. By 2pm it was full. The girls waved scarves and sang silly songs; the boys pushed each other into the girls and stole their scarves. Inspired by James, Miss Buckwell was wearing a multi-coloured traffic cone on her head. The away fans from Mayview had turned out in numbers also. There must have been at least a hundred adults and kids spread out along the opposite touchline, basking in the afternoon sun.

James sat in the dressing room silently, watching the other players taping shin pads around calves, tying boot laces, slipping boots on that didn't need laces. The 'Three Lions' song played on Omar's phone, reminding him of Dad. Was it a sign? A subliminal message wishing him good luck? He crumpled his nose. Probably not. Dad had no idea what James was up to, and he didn't know Omar's phone number. The song was about disappointment and hope. The hope of winning football's ultimate prize for the second time. And that hope always defeats the endless disappointment of never quite achieving it. Now HE had a chance to bring home the lost trophy. The only cup England had ever won. Bobby Moore had held that trophy, along with Pele and countless other heroes. Now he, James Eligus, could join them. Margot plonked herself down next to him and handed him a plastic bag.

'I got you a prezzie. They're not new, but I've only worn them a few times 'cos they were a bit tight.'

Rummaging in the bag, James took out a pair of new, and very cool-looking gold boots.

'Ah thanks Margot. I got something for you, too. Not as cool, but I went to Londis this morning.' He delved in his bag and tipped a handful of sweets into her palms. 'Thanks for helping me. I couldn't have done any of this without you.'

She leaned across and gave him a hug. The rest of the team, except for Shane and the two Buzzcut brothers, whistled and cheered and teased them both. Then Mr Smith walked in and delivered his team talk.

To begin, the emphasis was on quick, give-and-go passing.

'Find the spaces down the channels and trust each other. When we lose possession get in your blocks and press them. You're a good footballing team and you can beat this lot. So, trust yourselves and each other. Now get out there and show the world what you can do!'

There was a great roar from the dressing room as the door opened and The St Mark's team, wearing their customary red shirts and white shorts, filed out of the dressing room, clattered across the playground and made their way down the bank and onto the sunny pitch. As they lined up officially next to their counterparts from Mayview school, in white shirts and black shorts, the noise was pulsating.

Chapter 60

The match commentator, Clive Spillesly, in his customary sheepskin coat (yes, even in thirty degrees Celsius!) sat high above the pitch in a crane cabin. So, without further ado, let's hand over to him now.

'And welcome to a very sunny St Mark's Primary School in West London for this intriguing Year Six Interschools Cup Final between reigning champions Mayview, and first-time finalists St Mark's. We've got a full house here this afternoon, most of whom are noisily supporting the home team. Mayview arrive here today as hot favourites. No less than five of the starting nine players also play for big Premier League clubs, so they'll be used to the occasion. Only one from St Mark's plays for their county and that's Margot, but it's worth pointing out that she's also the Scotland captain in her age group so she's definitely one to look out for. To remind you there will be two halves of twenty minutes apiece, with nine players on each team and three substitutions allowed. The referee has called both captains across to the centre spot for the toss; Margot in the red of St Mark's and Casper Callaghan in the Mayview white. The crowd levels rise as Margot and Omar get us underway.'

2 mins

'Oh dear, Omar played a loose ball there and it's been picked up by Sasha for Mayfield who runs at the defence. Shane goes charging in and, oooh, that was awful. A dreadful challenge by Shane Splatter there. He went in with his studs showing and he could be in trouble, here. No, the referee settles for a warning. Shane is very lucky. But here comes the free kick. Sasha, she's got a very cultured left foot and Banksy, the St Mark's 'keeper, will have his work cut out.'

'She runs up and… GOAL TO MAYFIELD! That's the opener. A wonderful curling effort by Sasha into the top left corner! 1-0, and you have to say they deserved that.'

5 mins

'And it's Mayfield on the attack again. St Mark's haven't been allowed to get into their stride at all. It's Luther, flying down the wing. He left Omar for dead there. He's looking for a runner and plays it inside to Sasha who beats Shane to it and 2-0! What a finish from this young Arsenal academy player. A lovely low shot buried into the corner from just outside the box and this is comfortable for Mayfield already.'

9 mins

'Well, the St Mark's fans are getting a little bit restless here. Their team really hasn't got going at all. Sasha breaks free and she's charging towards goal. There's only Shane to beat and…good tackle. He kept his eye on the ball and won possession back for St Mark's and… Oh dear. All he had to do was pass it forward to Margot or Rekha, but he decided to shoot from his own half, and it's gone out for a throw in.'

Mayfield continued to dominate. St Marks were a shambles. Margot was floundering in midfield and the rest of the team looked shell shocked. To make matters worse, every time Shane won the ball or picked up a pass in his own area, he shot for goal.

HALF TIME

Chapter 61

The half time whistle couldn't come soon enough for Mr Smith. Calling his team in a circle around him, he stamped his feet angrily.

'What was that? It was an embarrassment, that's what that was! We're four-nil down and it could have been more. Banksy's the only one playing well and he's in goal. Shane, if you shoot once more from your own box, I'll substitute you straight away. You're part of a team. A team is a group of people who work for each other, help each other, fight for each other. Now, look up, pass the ball, and trust your teammates. If they make a mistake, encourage them.'

He clapped his hands passionately.

'Blonde Buzzcut, you're coming off. James, you're on.'

Shane groaned. The teacher glared at him.

'Got a problem with that?' The giant boy shook his head and looked down. 'Good.'

The teacher turned his attention to the small substitute. 'Find those spaces behind the defence and run at them. Now come on St Mark's, let's put on a show this half.'

The players clapped enthusiastically and fanned out across their half of the pitch. James's heart thudded in his chest. It felt like his legs had been swapped with two great tubes of jelly. He tried jogging on the spot and nearly fell over. Across the pitch, high above in the clear blue sky was Clive, the commentator, peering down from his metal nest at the top of the crane. Below him, the red and white St Mark's fans sat on the bank, bored and disappointed. Miss Buckwell had taken off her traffic cone hat and a group of boys were shouting rude noises through it. Up ahead was the pristine goal his team would attack this half. The tall opposition goalie stood between the sticks, jumping from side to side making it look impenetrable. He glanced along the touchline at the long line of flip-flops and trainers belonging to the noisy Mayfield fans, feeling certain one would trip him up. Then there were all the box-like TV cameras pointing at him like missile launchers from every corner. How many people were watching this rubbish, anyway? What if another ball fell on his head again? Or his shorts fell down, or he suddenly forgot how to kick? And why was it so hot? Feeling light-headed, he dropped down on all fours and felt the warm grass between his fingers.

'I see the sub looks like he needs subbing,' said a nearby Mayfield fan.

'Have you seen the size of him?' said another. 'Looks like they recruited him from the playgroup.'

'You ok, James?' said Margot, patting him on the back. He lifted his head.

'Do you think Shane might have swapped my legs with some flamingo's?'

Margot grinned. 'You're just nervous. Get up and take some deep breaths.'

'I can't walk.'

'Oh, stop being dramatic.'

She helped him to his feet and led him through a few deep breaths. 'There are thousands of people watching on telly, and you might win the World Cup that no-one's seen in a million years.'

'That's not really making me feel any better, Margot.'

She grabbed his shoulders. 'When will you ever get this chance again?'

He frowned. 'Never.'

'Never, aye. So, make the most of it, and let's go and have some fun.' He nodded, feeling a little brighter, and made his way to the edge of the centre circle.

Chapter 62

Now back to Clive in the commentary box.

2nd HALF

'One change now for St Mark's as Mayview get the second half underway. One of the Buzzcut brothers has been replaced by James Eligus on the left wing. He's a tiny player but he certainly looks the part with his long hair pushed back like Jack Grealish. Let's see if his skills can match up to his fashion sense.'

22 mins

'St Marks have started sloppily again. Sasha drives forward leaving James for dead. The poor sub looks like he has lead in his boots. One more goal would surely seal it for the visitors. She plays a neat one-two with Luther and hits a first time shot… Oh that's a wonderful acrobatic save from Banksy, diving high to his left to tip the ball round the post for another Mayview corner.'

24 mins

'St Marks are slowly getting back into this. They've pushed higher up the pitch and enjoying more possession.

Margot's starting to pull the strings in midfield and Shane has stopped shooting from his own house. The nerves certainly look like they've got the better of James Eligus, though. He can't control the ball, he can't sprint, he seems completely lost out there.'

'Now, here's a throw to the home team on that far side. It's just inside the Mayview half and Margot goes over to take it. She's dropped the ball and called James over. She's whispered something in his ear, and he's nodded. Now, he'll take the throw short, to Margot. He's made a run down the touchline, and she's found him. Now, James, looking more assured, looks up, ball at his feet, defender jockeying on the edge of the area. He plays a solid ball across to Margot who crosses for Omar at the far post and the keeper palms it wide for a corner. The substitute is going to take it over on the far side. He wipes his hands on his shorts and looks up. James is left-footed, so it'll be an outswinger. It's a solid kick that beats the first defender and Margot…scores! With a scissor kick! Outrageous. That's woken the fans up!'

Lost Trophy Challenge latest score: James 23 – Shane 21

28 mins

'There's a loose ball and James is first to it, driving down that far touchline. Marek, the Mayfield right back lunges in with the tackle but James has turned back the other way with a Cruyff turn. He's got space to cross, which he does, low and hard. The ball's bouncing around the Mayfield penalty box and Omar swings a boot at it and…it's in! It took a huge deflection to wrong foot the keeper, but St Mark's won't care about that. It's 4-2! Omar's so excited he's run straight across to the home fans and disappeared. His teammates look utterly baffled. No, he's back, and wearing what looks like a multicoloured traffic cone on his head. Extraordinary scenes! Now, one of the teachers has run on the pitch and taken it off him. Now she's parading around with it on. Incredible!'

30 mins

'Mayfield can't keep hold of the ball. What a spell of pressure this is from St Mark's. Now Shane's won possession by the centre circle. He passes forward to Margot, who nutmegs one, rainbow flicks over another, knocks it wide to Omar who hits a first time cross to Shane at the far post, who heads it back and Margot slides in to make it 4-3! Oh, incredible. What a comeback. What a second half performance!'

LTC latest score: James 25 – Shane 23

31 mins

'The reigning champions can't quite believe what's happening. Nevertheless, they restart the match with a pass wide to Marek. Ooh, he's taken a heavy touch and James has pounced on the loose ball again. St Mark's players surge forward. It's a full-on siege out there. The crowd roar James on down that far wing as he looks up and spots Shane belting forward from defence. He plays a defence-splitting pass and Shane rushes onto it, takes a touch and lashes the ball into the top corner. It's the equalizer! Amazing scenes here at St Mark's Primary School! Shane Splatter, who was utterly dreadful in the first half, has rescued his team, heroically! He disappears under a huddle of players and fans away to our right. Breath-taking, absolutely breath-taking.'

LTC latest score: James 25 – Shane 27

As the team headed back for the restart, Shane jogged across to James. His face had transformed. He had eyes and James noticed they were blue. His smile was almost inviting.

'Played James.' He acknowledged with a nod. 'I'm beating you by two, and there's two minutes left. You'd better not score.'

James wasn't sure if he was joking or not.

'You can set me up for the winner, though.' He slapped the small boy's ponytail and ran back to his position, pumping his fists to the crowd.

33 mins
'Just listen to the St Mark's fans now!'

We're gonna win the cup
We're gonna win the cup
And now you're gonna believe us
And now you're gonna believe us
And now you're gonna believe us
We're gonna win the cup!

'With a minute to go there's all to play for. Mayview have the ball, midway inside the St Mark's half. Sasha, so potent in the first period, charges forward. She passes to Luther, just outside the box with his back to goal. He turns, passes it back to Sasha. We're into the last minute. Now, across to the Callaghan boy on the right. Good possession this. Back to Sasha who loses her marker and she's in the box and… hits the post. The ball's still loose. Those Mayview fans thought they'd won it. Finally, it's hacked away up field by Omar. Chasing the high ball is James, who gets it under control and looks ahead. He's all alone with two defenders and the keeper between him and the goal. His socks are round his ankles, ponytail swaying behind, shorts eight sizes too big. He starts one of those mazy runs. Marek twists left and right trying to stay on his feet but the winger's got past him. The crowd are on their tiptoes. Here comes the other centre back and James knocks the ball to the left while running past the defender on the right. Now he's in the box with only the keeper to beat. He's rushed off his line and James flicks it over his outstretched leg and…Oh he's caught him. Surely that's a penalty? The St Mark's players plead with the referee. James is still on the floor. And he's given it! It's a penalty in the last minute to St Mark's.'

Chapter 63

On the pitch, it was chaos. James slowly got up as socks and boots tussled around him; fingers pointed angrily; heated words were exchanged. He stayed out of it, on the edge of the penalty box. Eventually, the referee, Mori, waved all-comers away and positioned himself a few metres from the penalty spot. Margot handed James the ball, but Shane had other ideas.

'It's mine. I'm taking it.'

'But James won the pen. He should take it.'

'He'll miss.'

James gritted his teeth and snatched the ball.

'I'm taking it' he insisted, placing it on the penalty spot.

James and Shane, short and tall, stared daggers at each other. With the ball on the spot and the ref in position with his whistle in his mouth, the rivals took one, two steps back, never taking their eyes off each other. James lining up to the right of the ball, Shane to the left. A quick glance at the ball, then to the ref. When he blew the whistle, it would be a straight sprint between them. The first to the ball could score and win the trophy. It was all down to this. James knew Shane was more powerful, but were his reactions quicker? He would soon find out. The substitute heard his dad's voice in his head.

'Pick a side and stick to it. Keep it low, James. Keep your head over the ball. Pass it in with your instep. Don't change your mind.'

He chose his side, the bottom right corner, and took a deep breath. With a stance like he was about to start a race, he eyed the ref like a hawk and waited, heart thudding in his ears, beating like a drum in his chest. Then...

PHRRREEP.

He sprang forward. THUD, THUD, THUD and struck the ball hard with his instep, head kept low. He lost balance and fell backwards, perhaps overcompensating for the almighty clattering he was expecting from Shane's boot. But it never came. Wait, what?

He heard a dink as the ball struck the post. Why could he only see sky? The glorious, wall to wall blue sky with all that space? Hang on, had he been in this position before? He squinted and held his breath, waiting for a second dizzying thump on the head.

Instead, he found himself being pounced on by a dozen ecstatic bodies as his senses returned. What he missed was this: The ball had hit the post. James had fallen backwards and bashed his head on the turf. Meanwhile, the ball ricocheted back off the post, hit the keeper on the side of the head and nestled in the back of the net.

A deafening roar. A mind-numbing scream! Mori, the referee blew his whistle. It was the end. St Mark's had won the match 5-4. James had won the Jules Rimet trophy.

Lost Trophy Challenge final score: James 29 – Shane 27

Chapter 64

As the team waited in line to pick up the silver cup, James tapped a strangely elated Shane on the shoulder. 'Why didn't you try and take the penalty?'

Shane grinned. 'If I'd won, my grandad would have stolen the cup. Plus, I heard he got your dad sent to prison, so...' There was a pause. 'Well played.' He held out a huge hand, which James shook, warmly. 'I'm gonna tell everyone I tweaked my hamstring going for the ball. You'd better back me up.' The boys shared a wry smile.

Mrs De'Ath, stood behind a desk by the centre circle, handed the silver cup, complete with red and white ribbons handed the silver cup, complete with red and white ribbons, to captain Margot. She thrust it high into the sunlit afternoon air, sparking wild celebrations on and off the pitch. Streamers and tinsel showered the players as they posed with the cup, singing:

'*Champions, Champions,*

Ole!, Ole!, Ole!'

Even Shane joined in. In fact, he looked like he was having more fun than James, who had spent most of the presentation looking around for a little old lady carrying the Jules Rimet under her arm. By the time the team had finished their lap of honour and the TV crew had started packing up their equipment, James had all but given up his search.

But then, appearing from high in the sky, was a sight that defied his eyes; a little old lady in a bright yellow coat flying a jetpack.

'Woohoo, James!' she called, lowering down over the centre circle.

At the same time, a police car screeched to a halt in the playground and two female officers sprinted down the bank carrying a black briefcase. The dwindling crowd rushed back forming a boisterous circle around Carlita, as the young officers helped her out of the jetpack and into a chair on the centre spot. Bringing the desk close, they presented her with the briefcase and stood to attention behind her.

A memory rushed back as James watched the old woman compose herself. Her face was unmistakable. He remembered asking, at Grandad's funeral, if she was famous because she looked so glamorous: with flawless cocoa skin, perfect sparkling teeth and almond shaped mahogany eyes. She had introduced herself as a long-lost friend and even given him a present after the service; a Brazil top, that was it!

Pushing back the mass of grey curls piled on top of her head, lowering her sunglasses and applying deep red lipstick, Carlita summoned the two contestants with a beckoning finger.

'Well done, boys!' she said, in her silky, Brazilian tone.

'You played a wonderful battle, especially the final. I enjoy this very much.' She turned to Shane. 'But why did you leave the penalty?'

The two lads looked at each other, knowingly.

'He tweaked his hamstring in the run up.' said James.

'I see. Now, Shane. The police would like to speak to you about your grandfather.'

He frowned. 'That selfish waste of space? He belongs in prison. I'll do all I can to help.'

'But where will you live if he's gone?' said James.

'My mum and dad are coming back from their cruise. But I think we should get out of that mansion, 'cos Measure the Treasure's buried, mate!'

The small boy smiled as Carlita turned to him.

'After the presentation, the police will take me to prison, and in return, your father will be released. Not immediately, it will take a little time, but soon.'

His eyes widened.

'Dad's getting out?'

The news hit him like a juggernaut. He had dreamed of this moment for two years and always seen himself running around deliriously. But now it was real, he didn't know how to react. Shane gave him a nudge and told him to cheer up. It was only then that a broad smile began to grow on his face.

Carlita leaned in secretively.

'I would have handed myself in and tried to free your dad, even if you'd lost.'

She then cleared her throat and addressed the crowd.

'Boys and girls, for the past two weeks these boys' – she nodded towards James and Shane – 'have been competing in my secret competition to win the World Cup.' The crowd murmured disbelievingly. 'You may not think I speak the truth, but here is proof.'

She turned the briefcase towards them revealing the solid gold Jules Rimet trophy. A huge gasp rang out.

'So, the winner of this trophy, after a remarkable battle, is James Eligus.'

Carlita carefully removed the gleaming trophy, clasping it at the base.

'This boy has shown kindness, courage, teamwork, and a desire to win against all odds. Plus, a little bit of luck. This is what you need to win the World Cup and it's why I present this to you now, James. Congratulations.'

With his hands trembling, James clasped the gleaming trophy and held it up to great cheers. It was heavier than he thought, but just the most beautiful thing he'd ever held in his entire life. Everything about it was perfect, from her toes to the delicate contours of her wings.

Clive reported the event live to the world. As James gazed at the beautiful trophy held high in his hands, he thought of his dad. The wings sparkled and shimmered in the sunshine giving the impression it was about to take flight. Hopefully, one day soon, Dad would find his wings too. But then his fantasy was cut off by a familiar voice

Chapter 65

'Shane! Did you win?' Brett Splatter, dressed in a yellow and green tracksuit, hurried across the pitch towards them, waving his hands in the air.

'Is it ours? Did you win?'

Shane shook his head. 'James won, fair and square.'

Spotting the trophy, he shoved his grandson out the way. 'Is that, er…?'

James nodded. 'This is the real trophy. Nothing like your rubbish fake.'

He coughed nervously, spotting the officers, and nodded to the old woman.

'So, you must be the elusive Carlita.' He shot her a sickly smile.

'That's right.'

A fixed grin had etched itself across his round, sweaty face.

'Well, I must say, you're the absolute king of the hide and seekers.'

'Queen' Carlita corrected him.

'I didn't even know what you looked like! You're pretty. Pretty old! Ha.'

'At least I'm not pretty ugly, like you, Mr Splatter!'

He went up to one of the officers and prodded her on the arm.

'Have you ever searched for something for forty years?'

'Don't do that, sir.'

'Sorry, it's just that…' He gazed at the trophy once again and his expression turned to longing. 'I love you, dear Julie.' He reached over to grab it, but James held it close, shielding it away from the nasty man.

'I think that's enough, sir.'

'May I hold her, James? Before you take her away?' He asked like a street urchin begging for bread.

James looked to Carlita, who cocked her head to one side; then to the police officer, who frowned; then to Shane, who nodded reluctantly and finally, to Margot. However, in a moment of sheer defiance, Brett Splatter snatched the trophy, sent the cameraman toppling over and made a run for it across the grass, holding it high in the air.

'You'll never catch me!'

Margot picked up the match ball and was about to unleash a shot to knock the old man down. But Shane had another idea. Throwing the ball out in front of him, he hoofed the ball as hard and as high as he could. This time, however, they followed its trajectory with a jog that also kept them close to Brett Splatter and the precious trophy.

'This is like before,' said Shane.

'When?' Said James.

'When it landed on you.'

'We didn't recognise you at the time,' said Margot.

'It's because you were called FA Cup' added Omar.

'And your hair was long' said Banksy.

'Still is' said James.

'The ball's stopped' said Margot.

'It's coming down' said Omar.

'Where do you think it's going to land?' said James.

'Somewhere special, hopefully' said Shane.

'If you make this shot, I'll bring you to Scotland for trials' said Margot.

'I ain't playing for them!'

'It's gonna hurt like mad!' said James.

'That's the idea' said Shane. 'Oi, Grandad! Look up!'

With a satisfying SPPPPFFFFFTTT, the ball landed directly on top of Brett Splatter's head and settled gently around his ears. He toppled to the floor with a groan as the trophy bounced out of his hands and landed safely at James' feet.

Chapter 66

Hanwell's new reluctant celebrity spent the following day answering questions from news crews and journalists from across the globe, sparking these headlines.

IT'S FINALLY COME HOME!

**AFTER OVER HALF A CENTURY,
AN ENGLISHMAN BRINGS FOOTBALL
HOME AGAIN**

**DON'T FAINT, BUT ENGLAND
WIN WORLD CUP (BUT HE'S GIVING
IT BACK TO BRAZIL!)**

James was whisked off to Wembley Stadium for a photoshoot with some of the surviving 1966 squad and showed Geoff Hurst a recreation of his famous crossbar goal on the Wembley pitch. He kept the trophy in his room on the lid of his stereo to keep it away from Auntie Sue and her allergy. During the day, he'd take it to the park where he, Margot, Omar and Shane, played matches against other local kids. The winners did laps of honour

After his time with the trophy was over, James showed

the police into the Nerve Centre and let them take anything they wanted, which was almost everything. He was interviewed and interrogated, apologised to and rewarded with a lifetime's worth of free tickets to all England matches, which he thought was pretty cool.

Carlita was taken to an open prison where she took up gardening, relieved at not having to hide any more. And auntie Sue became something of a TV celebrity, appearing on numerous morning shows as Britain's first person to be allergic to football.

EPILOGUE

Four months later.

It was one of those days when the rain and wind were having a battle to see who was better. The autumn leaves didn't know which side to support so they had a chat and decided auntie Sue's windscreen was the best place to rest. The wipers swished in rhythm to the song on the radio as James fidgeted in the passenger seat. With every passing mile the knot in his stomach grew, but this time he knew that it wasn't because of Fleurbler.

As the high walls of the prison appeared before them, James suddenly had a series of dreadful thoughts: what if dad wasn't allowed out? What if he didn't want to be free? What if he'd become content and liked it in there? Like a bear in hibernation? Auntie Sue parked the car, put an arm round him and told him to stop being silly.

They were led into an empty courtyard and told to wait. It was deathly quiet, apart from the howling wind. An armoured vehicle pulled up next to them. The man in the back was dragged out wearing handcuffs. His voice was annoyingly familiar.

'Stop tugging, you oafs. Don't you know who I am? I'm the world-famous Brett Splatter.'

He caught sight of James and went purple with rage. 'This is all your fault, Eligus!'

The guards told him to apologise. He refused. They shrugged and told him, in that case, he'd be cleaning the toilets for the next five years. The old man began sobbing as they led him across the courtyard towards a big steel door.

As the door slowly opened, a screech echoed around the courtyard. James held his breath, his eyes fixed on the doorway in the distance. A shadow flickered, then a glimpse of a bag and the sounds of 'good luck, George.' And finally, there he was, standing tall, taking in the fresh air of freedom, wearing the same navy suit James had last seen him in all those years ago. Dad. He wanted to run to him, across that courtyard, past the malignant creature who had caused all this harm. But a guard appeared next to his father and auntie Sue told him to be patient.

Brett Splatter and George Eligus passed each other halfway across the yard; one walking to his smiling family, the other towards a future of cleaning poo. The old man couldn't resist one last swipe at his enemy. 'This ain't over, Eligus! I always win!'

James' father grinned. 'You might have beaten me, but you've just lost to a ten-year-old. All the lads inside are really looking forward to meeting you. Especially after what you said about us English people.'

The former game show host was led away, kicking and screaming as James' dad raced towards his son wearing a smile the size of a football pitch. James gulped, his heart fit to burst as they hugged each other, tightly. This feeling was better even than winning the World Cup.

'Hello Dad.' he said.

THE END

ACKNOWLEDGEMENTS

To Steve Bacon, Mark Underwood and Simon Konecki for your unwavering support and help with the story. To Bobby Birchall, Chris Waterlow, Silvia Molteni and Mike Lomon for all your time and expertise; Peter Briley and St Marks' Primary for letting me read to you; to my social media gurus, Prisha Barua and Charlotte Bowden; to Chip for putting up with my edits! To all my friends and family for your love and motivation. Finally, to Selina, Rudi and Tia for, well, pretty much everything.

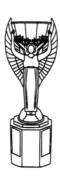